ONE

ETTA WATCHED from the second story, dusty, gray window as the carriage pulled up to the front of her home. She wiped at the layer of filth, which allowed her to see what she most feared. Her stomach clenched in knots as a gentleman stepped out into the fog and light mist of rain. He placed the black hat atop his head, shielding himself from the moisture.

Henrietta wanted to hide. She had not seen her Uncle Jack since she had been a little girl, no older than five. At the time, he had scared her; his putrid breath and leering stare. He had even made a joke about her betrothal, something she hadn't wanted to think about as a child, let alone now, fifteen years later.

Her mother had passed away in childbirth, and her father had perished just last week, leaving everything, including his only daughter, to a brother he had not kept in touch with in well over a decade.

She had no desire to leave her residence but she herself had no money, the dowry being tied up with her Uncle Jack, which meant it would be her time to leave soon—and leave everything she knew behind.

Her travel satchel sat on the mattress in her bedroom, next to where her single trunk stood full and ready. Henrietta had packed by herself at the news of her departure, all servants already having been discharged. Would she be given adequate accommodations when she reached her uncle's home? Or would he lock her in a cellar, the way he did in her paranoid nightmares?

Etta had always had an overactive imagination, or so she had been told. Stories flowed freely from her lips, embellishments easy to make as she envisioned a unique world and fascinating tales of witches and sorcery. Her amused father had insisted the stories remain between them, that even so much as a hint of her wild narratives could cause her to find herself in an unfortunate situation. At the very least, he had told her, it was quite improper for a lady to have such thoughts. She had been cautious, of course, trusting very few people and having even less friends over the years as her father grew ill and she spent her later years caring for him.

At twenty, she was of an age to marry, but her prospects lacked in bounty—in fact, they were lacking altogether. If she were to be honest, Etta found pleasure in being free. The responsibility of such a commitment, a contract between two people and the exchange of a dowry for her hand, felt wickedly absurd. However, it was not as though she could voice such a sentiment to anyone.

Fear crept inside her. Etta's hands shook with nerves as her uncle stepped inside the house. She could hear his footfall through the floorboards down below.

"Henrietta!" he called, his deep voice echoing off the walls. He stood in the foyer, making no attempt to wander any further inside.

With caution, she edged out of her room and stood at the top of the stairs, staring down the banister to the ground floor at Uncle Jack. He had not changed much since she had last seen him, except perhaps he had grown a little older, his dark black hair now showing wisps of gray. He was taller than her father, yet her uncle's posture gave him the appearance of being hunched forward, along with his protruding potbelly. As she continued to stare at him, she realized he looked nothing like his brother, except for the slightly hooked nose, a trait that all men in the family had acquired.

"Please, sir, I prefer to be called Etta," she said. "My trunk is up here."

"You will answer to what I call you, Henrietta. Bring your belongings downstairs. The road is wet, and we do not wish to ride at night."

She knew what he really meant—that if she did not make haste, he'd be forced to stay at the house for the evening and, for whatever reason, he was not going to do that.

"Yes, of course." Etta stepped into her bedroom and lifted one end of the trunk by the thick leather handle, dragging it across the red and yellow rug and over the wooden floor and down the stairs, listening to it smack each stair on its descent down.

She prayed it would not leave scratches on the perfectly sanded floorboards. The grain was as beautiful as it had been the day it was constructed, or so she imagined. The house had many years to it, as her father had moved in long before she had been born.

Jack cleared his throat, perhaps expecting Henrietta to lift the trunk and carry it properly, an impossibility, of course. If the trunk had not weighed close to what she herself did, she would have found it easier to transport down the stairs.

"You are bringing all that?" he asked, staring at her as if she had gone insane. He shook his head. "Come, Henrietta. We have not got all day." He stepped outside and left the front door open.

The moment weighed heavily on her; leaving behind the only home she'd ever known. The hinges to the door had rusted, an oversight she'd had when tending to the house and her ailing father. She'd heard the constant squeak and groan of the rusted metal whenever she let the doctors in to visit, but as quickly as the sound reminded her, the thought would be forgotten at her father's groans and coughs.

In the earlier years of his sickness, she'd been keeping up with the chores, making sure the house looked beautiful for him. More recently, her focus had been set entirely on her father. She had no regrets, except that she didn't have more time to spend with him.

Etta glanced over her shoulder, already missing the warmth and smells of her home terribly, but the house was no longer the same without her father. Even in his last dying moments, she'd kept the place up as best she could, lighting candles and sprinkling cinnamon into the flames to ward off the stench of death. The house needed a fresh coat of paint and a few shingles had come loose, but there were worse places to live. The memories seeped into her with every glance at the walls, the paintings a reminder of her father's talent. She wanted to take one with her, but she could not carry it as well as her trunk. Would Jack sell the paintings and the house? Would the treasures of her past be scattered amongst the townsfolk for a few shillings?

Following her uncle outside, she used all her strength to lift the trunk just a smidge from the ground, awkwardly trying to keep her travel satchel balanced over her shoulder, hoping to prevent it from falling to the soft soil. Etta hated December weather, with the cool temperatures forcing her to keep her cloak pulled tight around her body. Her hands grew red and numb as she struggled toward the carriage.

Uncle Jack waited beside the coach, finally snapping at the driver to assist Etta with her belongings, then reaching out to aid her inside. She stumbled forward, grabbing a seat across from him. To her, he felt like a stranger, even though they were bound by blood. Her father and Jack had not seen one another in years. She did not know the exact reason why they'd had a falling out and her father, even on his deathbed, had not uttered the words to tell her what her fate would be.

In fact, her father had not given her any indication that Uncle Jack would be her guardian. It had been the lawyer who arrived that had informed her she now belonged to a relative—along with her dowry and the house. She herself had nothing.

"I am sorry to inform you, Miss Waters, but your father wished for his brother to have the house and to look after his only daughter. His will states that Mr. Jack Waters is

the sole heir, and your dowry will be paid to a husband of his choosing."

"You can't be serious," Etta had said, her heart slamming against the walls of her chest. "My father has not spoken to Uncle Jack since I was a child. When was the will drawn up?" Perhaps he had not got around to making the necessary changes.

"That does not matter, Miss Waters." The lawyer had sighed, shifting his hat slightly atop his bulbaceous head. His eyebrows were thick and met just above the line to his nose. A few wisps of gray hair edged from the gentleman's nostrils, making him rather unappealing for a man a decade younger than her father. "I know this is troubling for you, as you are of an age to wed, but perhaps this is for the best. You have spent many years caring for your dying father, is that not correct?"

Etta did not agree that it was for the best, but yes, she had stayed at her father's bedside while he had withered away, the ghost of what eventually killed him dragging him between life and death for years. "Yes, I stayed with him. I was his nurse." Though she did not know much about being a nurse, she had acquired enough skills to feed him with a spoon and roll him around often to keep him from acquiring bedsores. She had carefully utilized all information provided by the doctor who had visited him twice a week.

"Just as you cared for your father, your uncle will care for you," the lawyer had said. His no nonsense tone told her that arguing would do little good. "I am sure he will be anxious to find you a suitable husband. Let your uncle take care of you, Miss Waters. It is what your father wanted."

The ride to her uncle's estate was cloaked in silence. The clank of the wheels and the horses' hooves pounding the earth were the only sounds that reached Etta's ears. She did not know what would become of her when she set foot inside his home. Would he expect her to cook and clean for him? Did he intend to marry her off immediately? She folded her hands together in her lap, anxiously waiting for her uncle to say something—anything. She was met with silence.

"We're here." His voice seemed to carry with the wind as she stared out of the carriage window. They were approaching a house larger than her father's by far. The three story structure sent a shudder down her spine; the way its dark, gray stones loomed high above. It towered over Etta, making her feel incredibly small and unwanted due to its massive size. The lawn extended as far as the eye could see, perfectly manicured, with groundskeepers likely caring for the land. Etta doubted her uncle went outside and pruned the bushes, ever. He didn't seem the type to get his hands dirty, at least when it came to the soil outside. She certainly couldn't speak for his character.

"What is your profession, Uncle Jack?" It was a rude question, but she could not fathom how he could afford such a luxurious home and lifestyle.

"I am a businessman," he said. His answer was short and to the point, offering no hint of what that meant exactly.

Etta sat in silence as the driver pulled the carriage around to the front of the home. Once they'd drawn to a stop, he came around to open the door. He offered his hand, and Etta grabbed it, as well as her satchel.

When her eyes went toward her trunk, he smiled. "Allow me," he said, taking her trunk up to the door.

The front door swung open wide, and an older woman who could have easily been Uncle Jack's wife opened the door. "You must be Miss Henrietta," she said. "Here, I shall have your belongings brought to your room. Remove your cloak and then join us for dinner."

"Please call me Etta," she said, correcting the woman who hadn't given her name. Etta followed her inside the house and slipped out of her cloak, leaving it in the foyer—the house was warm and comfortable enough that she didn't need it. The house smelled funny, though, like an old man's sock drawer. The scent tickled her nose in the most unappealing way. She opted to breathe through her mouth and prayed she might soon be able to open a window to let some fresh air into her new home.

Etta's eyes moved over the bare walls. Not a single painting had been hung up, which was a peculiar sight for a girl who had grown up with a love of art. The candlelight reflected off the walls, revealing a lackluster gray color, most unappealing to the eye. She stared up at the high-vaulted ceilings. The stairwell climbed around the room, and she swallowed nervously. She would surely get lost before the night was over. Already she felt overwhelmed and saddened, missing her father more than she had since the moment he had passed.

Unwilling to let her uncle see the despair in her eyes, she bit her bottom lip and sucked in the emotion, pretending to be pleased with the arrangement.

The woman pointed a firm finger upstairs to the driver, even though he seemed to know his way.

Etta stood in the foyer, hungry and praying her stomach wouldn't rumble and embarrass her. The last meal she'd eaten had been that morning, and had consisted of porridge. Food had been scarce lately, due to the lack of money since her father's passing. She had nothing, it had all been given to her uncle, which meant she had to trust he would take care of her. She hoped dinner would be soon, given the hour, though she was quite unsure where the dining room was located. Would they serve anything she might find appealing?

Uncle Jack followed her inside, stepping on the mat before he shed his coat and hat. "This way, Henrietta." He must have sensed her unease. "We shall be having company this evening. Seeing as how you are of legal age to marry, there is someone I would like you to meet; a business associate of mine, Philip Hartley."

Etta swallowed the lump in her throat. Business associate? Did that mean he was as old as her uncle? She did not dare voice her concerns. Jack had been kind enough to take her in, but it was clear he did not want her to stay for long. It was not as though she desired to be there either. They would have to make do with one another, for now.

TWO

PHILIP WENT UP THE STAIRS, his eyes taking in the manor. The place could never be called quaint—in fact it was large enough to house a princess, yet not fancy enough. Philip had grown comfortable with his surroundings at the Ashby Chateau. He may not have lived a life of luxury ever since he'd been born, but he had done well for himself, and indulged in the finer things that life had to offer. He had expected gas lamps to line the path on his way inside, but only a single light had been stationed at the gate upon his entrance, and it had burned out. The grounds, though tended to, ought to have been trimmed again more recently; the grass was too high for his liking. The stone walls could have resembled a castle, had the stone been scrubbed clean of the offending mold sprouting on the side of the building. Adjusting his coat, he knocked on the front door.

The housekeeper opened it, barely cracking it wide enough to peek around.

"Good afternoon, madam." He bowed his head in greeting. "Philip Hartley. I am here to see Mr. Waters."

"Good afternoon, sir. Please come inside. The master will be with you in a moment," the housekeeper said. She led him into the foyer and offered to take his top hat and coat.

"Thank you," he said, standing in the front hall, his eyes darting over the starkly bare walls and the large staircase that led to the first floor. The house was in pristine condition, as if no one had ever lived inside it. A strangeness surrounded the place, the smell being oddly familiar.

Philip knew Mr. Jack Waters from his business dealings. He had worked with him on law contracts, and offered guidance whenever Mr. Waters suspected he was being swindled. Jack had invited him to dinner, though he did not quite know what the occasion was. He rarely mixed business with pleasure, but upon Jack's insistence, he had agreed.

"It is a pleasure to see you again, Mr. Hartley," Jack said as he entered the foyer.

Philip smiled through tight lips. "There is no reason to be so formal. It is Philip." If they were here for dinner, then they surely may talk business, but he found no need for their conduct to be so tight and stuffy. Philip had friends, but very few outside of the community in which he lived. It was a nice change to be invited to dinner, especially one so elegant and formal. He hoped he had not under dressed for the occasion, in his white shirt, black trousers, and black striped waistcoat, with his tie tucked neatly down between his shirt and vest.

"Likewise. Come, we are ready to dine."

Philip raised an eyebrow, curious as to who else would be joining them for dinner. As far as he knew, Jack was not married and had no children. The man had several housekeepers who cared for his home, fed him a proper meal, and looked after him, but none that he was tied down to.

Philip followed Jack into the dining room and was quite surprised to see a lovely woman, a few years younger than him, sitting quietly and alone at the table. She was holding up her fork, glancing at her reflection in the silver. She looked quite lovely and nervous; her hand twitched at the realization that someone else had entered the room. Her long blonde hair flowed down her back and moved with her like a kiss from the wind, caressing her skin, as she turned her head to see what the commotion was all about.

As soon as her crystal blue eyes met his, she dropped the utensil on the table. It made a clanking sound as she pushed her chair back to stand.

"I do not believe we've met," Philip said, walking toward her, offering his hand. His eyes moved over her perfect creamy complexion and down to the dusting of freckles on her neck that dipped down to just above her breasts, where her gown prevented any further glimpse of her skin.

"My name is Etta Waters, sir."

Philip glanced from Etta to Jack. "You did not tell me you had a daughter."

"She is my niece," Jack said, quick to clarify his position. "My brother passed away a short time ago. Henrietta has come to live here with me, until I can find her a proper home. She has just arrived."

Philip's eyes narrowed. Had that been why Jack was quick to invite him? He wanted to marry the poor girl off? She was beautiful, no doubt, with her rosy cheeks and long blonde tresses, but he did not have time to look after a wife, especially one who was undoubtedly still grieving the loss of her father.

"I am not in need of a wife, Jack, if that was the implication of tonight's dinner."

"Of course not," Jack said, shaking his head. He took a seat at the table, waving his hand as if to dismiss such an idea. "I thought your new finishing school... Ashby Chateau, is it? I thought it might suit Henrietta perfectly."

"I prefer to be called Etta," she corrected firmly, yet still polite.

Jack shot a glare at *Etta* and then nodded toward Philip. "I believe it is quite clear what I mean."

Philip stared at the young blonde, considering the request. Nodding, he said, "Yes, I have recently opened a finishing school to prepare young ladies such as Miss Waters for marriage. Perhaps such an establishment would do a lady of her nature some good." He paused and studied the nervous young woman before him. Her mouth was open in shock, yet she remained quiet, even though she clearly wanted to speak. Turning his attention back to Jack, he added, "There would be, of course, a cost associated with her time at the Ashby Chateau."

"Yes," Jack said with a nod. "Whatever the cost, I would like her enrolled without delay."

"Are you expecting us to provide her with a suitable husband upon her graduation?" Philip asked. His eyes locked on the blonde. She looked scared to death, as if she was mere moments from bolting out of her chair. The poor young lady—just wait until she discovered what his finishing school was truly all about.

"It would be appreciated. I know you have men who come and frequent the chateau to find a dutiful and accomplished wife. Even though it's still early days, your establishment has already acquired quite the reputation. I would like to see Henrietta make a suitable marriage. She has a dowry, and I intend to increase it with the money from the sale of her father's estate."

"You cannot sell my home! I will not allow it!" Henrietta burst out, her eyes glistening with unshed tears.

An interesting response, thought Philip. What had she thought would happen to the property once it was vacated? Up until now, this woman had sat very docilely, and yet it was clear a fire burned behind that soft appearance. He liked it.

"We will, and you must settle yourself down at once," Jack snapped. "Or I will have you taken to the study and caned before dinner begins."

She wiped her tears with the back of her hand and pressed her lips together.

Philip cleared his throat before saying, "I see she could benefit from some time at Ashby Chateau." Henrietta fixed him with a murderous glare but said nothing more. "When were you anticipating enrollment of your niece?" Philip went on.

"Tomorrow would be preferable. Unless, of course, you have room in your carriage to bring her back with you this evening."

It seemed as though Jack did not want to waste a minute getting the young lady out of his care. Was she that difficult to manage, or had he no experience with women at all?

Henrietta did not say a word. Philip had not the slightest clue what was going through the young woman's mind. "She will ride with me and take only the clothes on her back," he said at length.

"My trunk is upstairs. It is already packed. You would not have to wait for me," Henrietta said. "I am prepared to leave when you are."

It surprised Philip that she did not argue about leaving her uncle behind, especially so soon after her arrival. Most girls kicked and screamed, throwing a temper tantrum at the first mention of finishing school. He suspected that Henrietta was not like most girls, though. It was quite clear that her submissive nature was in constant battle with her feisty one. Proper etiquette strangled her wild soul— her eyes revealed that secret. Perhaps he'd found himself a rare gem, a young woman for his own pleasure. It had been years since his first wife had passed on, and it was time he found himself a lady who would make him happy. Could it be Henrietta who would ease the pain and bring him such pleasure? Staring at the little fireball with her arms folded across her chest, her pouty lips in a firm line, Philip couldn't help but be amused by her defiance. She was a rough gem, at that, and would need the strictest upbringing from Nanny Mae to ensure she understood her place at the chateau.

"Your clothes will be provided by Ashby Chateau, Henrietta. I assure you, any possessions you bring will, in most cases, be withheld from you anyway. It is best if you come as you are," Philip said.

"May I ask what I will be learning at your finishing school?" Henrietta's brow furrowed. The staff entered the dining room carrying trays of food, placing the first course of the meal in front of the diners.

Noticing the fact that she had reached for the wrong fork, he answered, "For starters, when to use which fork." Philip smiled at her discomfort. "There is a special school for young women who show promise and I do believe that you, my dear, will fit in with little Gracie and Leda quite nicely. Perhaps I will introduce them to you tomorrow morning at breakfast."

"I want reassurances that my niece will be married upon graduation," Jack said. "If she does not marry, then I will expect a full refund for monies paid."

Philip exhaled heavily. He should have known Jack would be one of the more problematic clients; the type who were most difficult and caused him to dislike his job at least once a week. "I assure you that the only time you will hear from me again will be with regards to your niece's dowry."

"Good." Jack nodded, seeming satisfied with that response. He reached into his pocket for a handkerchief, wiping his brow that had been glistening with sweat.

Philip had a way of making a man nervous. He was not one of extreme power, such as Queen Victoria or even a soldier from the royal guard. Philip did, however, hold a great deal of wealth and property, and made his money investing in businesses across Britain. His strong build and dark features gave off an imposing aura, and many men lacked the temerity to meet him head on.

Henrietta waited until both gentlemen had selected the proper forks before she followed suit, and they ate dinner together. The room was bathed in an awkward silence, but Philip could see that Henrietta continued to sneak glances in his direction.

Philip had traveled several hours to arrive at Jack Waters' home, and would have several more of riding through the night to get back in time for tomorrow's lesson. Staying in an unfamiliar house was not an option for him. He preferred the comfort of the reliable and what he could count on, his own brand of family, which he himself had created.

His eyes danced up from his food to Henrietta. She had long thick black eyelashes that seemed both exotic and beautiful on her. They blanketed the crystal azure of her eyes. With her blonde hair, tiny frame, and sweet innocence, she very well could become his most prized pupil—with the proper training.

She caught him staring and blushed, not saying a word. She surprised him by not looking away, but bravely maintaining her glare.

Philip adverted his gaze, letting it drop to the salad he was picking at, not at all hungry. Travel never did him well, and he was in dire need of a good night's sleep.

"Tell me, Mr. Hartley, will I be given the opportunity to choose the man I wish to marry, as well?" She asked the question so sweetly, yet her eyes burned with insolence.

"Henrietta," her uncle warned. "Mind your place, young lady, or the cane will be awaiting your arrival."

She bit her lip, pushing the food around her plate as her eyes dropped to the table, evidently disappointed.

"We do try and make an appropriate match with regards to dowry and position. I assure you, this is what your father would have wanted for you," Philip responded, feeling as if her question deserved an answer.

Henrietta pushed her plate away. "You have no way of knowing that, Mr. Hartley. You never met my father."

"Henrietta!" Jack scolded his niece again.

"I am no longer hungry," she said. Pushing herself back from the table, she stood up.

"I did not excuse you, young lady." Jack's eyes narrowed, and his fist pounded the wooden table.

Philip watched the exchange between them. Was this her typical behavior, or did she not get along well with her uncle? He watched her with fascination as she stalked out of the room, stomping her feet in the process. A good hard spanking to her bottom would do her the world of good. However, it was not his place to do so... yet.

"Please tell me you will take her tonight," Jack all but growled. His jaw tightened as his control weakened.

"Of course," Philip said, nodding. "I shall draw up the paperwork as soon as we finish the meal. I assure you, Mr. Waters, your niece will be in very good hands. A proper education is just what she is in need of."

THREE

ETTA COULD NOT BELIEVE the gall of Mr. Hartley. How dare he think he knew what her father would have wanted! Her father was dead, and she felt quite certain that Mr. Hartley had never met him. Surely if he had, she would have known about it.

She stormed up the stairs, struggling to find her bedroom. Opening and slamming doors, she finally came to a room which contained a bed. Her trunk was on the floor. She flipped the lock, lifting its lid in a huff.

How could she go with this stranger so easily? Although he seemed far more charming than her uncle; who was obviously a poor excuse of a relative who seemed to want her gone at the first chance possible.

Why did she have to go to a finishing school, though? She knew how to wear a dress and pin up her hair. She'd spent enough time among friends in her younger years to know how to conduct herself like a lady. She may not be accomplished in all things; playing the piano, for instance, and her table etiquette was a bit rusty, but she was still far from in need of a finishing school.

Her father had been gravely ill since she had turned fifteen, and his decline had only grown more evident as the unkind years ticked by. At one point she had assumed he would never see her sixteenth birthday, and when he had awoken on that Saturday morning, she found it a miracle that he did indeed look better.

Her father had good days and bad. His health was on a constant decline, his memory fading in his later years, until he no longer recognized his daughter upon seeing her.

It saddened Etta; watching him die, unable to help him the way she had wanted to. Would this have been what her father wanted for her? To attend Ashby Chateau?

It did not sound so terrible compared to living with Uncle Jack. He barely seemed to say two words to her. Why did he hate her so much? What had she done to him as a child that made him resent her so?

Her fingers pushed through the mounds of clothes she had brought. How could she be expected to leave her possessions behind? It had been terrible enough leaving her home, and now she was being told to leave behind everything but the few clothes on her back as well?

Balling the dresses up into her fists, she threw them across the room, screaming as tears trickled down her face. "I hate him!" The words echoed through the room and most likely down the stairs. Could her uncle hear her fit of rage? Would he be angry about her displeasure toward him? He'd opened up his home to her and was paying for her to attend finishing school, though Etta assumed the money would be coming from her father's estate, once it had been sold.

"That is not a very nice thing to say," Philip said. He was standing outside the door.

Etta wiped the tears away. She had not known anyone had been watching her. "I thought you were still eating," she muttered.

"I do not have much of an appetite when I travel. The paperwork has been drawn up. All I have to do is sign, and you will come and join me at Ashby Chateau."

Etta sat on the floor, with nightgowns at her feet and dresses strewn throughout the room. What did he think of this display? Would he assume she behaved this way for attention? It had not been easy losing her father. To this day, the weight of the loss smothered her and made her feel as though she were drowning in a constant sea of misery.

"You have not signed yet?" she asked.

"I would like it to be your choice to attend, Etta."

She relaxed slightly at hearing him call her by the nickname her father had given her, for the first time. "How can I know what I want, when I do not understand what will be expected of me?"

"That is a good question. I assure you, many young ladies are brought in, most younger than you are. Which is why I want your acceptance. You will come downstairs and sign the contract with your uncle. It reads that you agree to attend, and that you will follow the rules of the establishment. Your uncle may control your assets but you are of legal age, Etta. I would like your consent, as well."

Surprised that he cared enough to ask, she nodded slowly. If she did not agree to go with him, would she still be forced to attend Ashby Chateau? What about her uncle? Would he keep her dowry and the money from her father's estate without giving her a penny? Jack certainly did not seem keen to have her, already wanting to see her whisked away on the very first night.

"I shall sign it," Etta said. What choice did she really have? Her family was gone. Maybe a new beginning, away from a man her father had not spoken to in over a decade, was a wise decision.

"Good girl." Philip smiled. "Now, come downstairs. We shall be leaving shortly after the contract is ready."

Etta stood and glanced back at the mess of gowns thrown haphazardly across the room. "I really can't bring any of it with me?" The thought of leaving the last of her things behind brought her to tears again.

Philip stepped into the room, his hands finding her arms. He stood there, staring deep into her eyes. "I assure you, you will not be needing those dresses at Ashby Chateau."

"And what about when I am married? I shall have nothing then."

"Your Uncle Jack will bring your gowns when he brings the dowry to your husband. Let him keep the dresses here for safe keeping. In fact, I will make a note of it in the contract, so he will be forbidden from destroying or selling the gowns."

Etta wiped the last of her tears away. "Thank you, Mr. Hartley. You have been incredibly kind to me."

"There is no reason to be any other way," he said. "Now come, let us go downstairs and finish up the paperwork so we may begin our journey."

She headed down the stairs first, waiting for him at the bottom, unsure where they were heading to sign the contract. Etta still had not become familiar with the house, and it seemed as though it would not matter. She would be leaving tonight, and she could forget her Uncle Jack as quickly as he would forget her.

FOUR

PHILIP WALKED down the front steps, the contract tucked neatly into an envelope and buried under his coat. Rain pelted his hat as he walked outside. He should have brought an umbrella, and Jack did not seem to be offering one.

Etta used her cloak to cover her head as she briskly walked to the carriage.

Philip assisted her in first and shut the door, noting that her uncle hadn't even bothered to bid her farewell as the driver steered them off the grounds and onto the main road. He closed the windows to the carriage, to keep the rain from splashing them as they drove. "Quite a night," he said.

"Yes." Thunder rumbled in the distance, and the horses continued trotting forward. "Do you think it is safe to travel tonight? Should we have waited until the storm passed?" she asked uncertainly.

"We need to be at the chateau before dawn. I wish it were that simple, Etta. But that is for me to worry about, not you." He watched lines of concern etch her brow, and oddly, he had the overwhelming desire to pull her into his arms and reassure her that she would be safe; that he would never allow anything or anyone to cause her harm. "Tell me, when was the last time you felt the innocence of being a child: carefree and without worry?" he asked gently.

Sighing and allowing her shoulders to collapse in a slump, she answered. "I do not remember ever being carefree and without worry, Mr. Hartley. I do not have the luxury in life to do so."

"Do you not wish sometimes that you could be like a child? Have no worries, no concerns of misfortune, and no hard decisions to make. Have you ever wished to have someone take care of you, fully take care of your every need? Have you ever wanted to be tucked in at night, kissed on the forehead and told to have sweet dreams, and you would, because someone who loves you very much has already chased the bad dreams away?"

She laughed softly under her breath. "I do not know. Why are you asking me such a peculiar question, Mr. Hartley?"

"I feel it is best to just be blunt and not skirt around the topic with regards to what is required of you at Ashby Chateau. Behavior, expectations, and beliefs are quite different there. We want to help you find that little girl that once was lost. We want you to rest easy and know that everything will be taken care of. *You* will be taken care of."

"Oh?"

"To begin with, I want you to call me 'Papa'. When we arrive at Ashby Chateau, Nanny Mae is going to get you ready for bed, but come the morning, we will educate you on what is to occur with your schooling."

"Papa?" She gave him the strangest look, as if he had gone mad, although she did not seem to find the suggestion offensive. "I do not need a nanny, Mr. Hartley. I am twenty years old. I also do not understand why you would want me to call you such a name."

Philip ignored her. "I know it will take some getting used to, little Etta, but your new school is going to teach you how not only to behave as a proper little wife, but to submit to a man in ways you cannot imagine at this time. Part of that training involves being little again."

"Little?"

"Do not worry yourself now about the details. Everything will be taken care of for you while you are at the Ashby Chateau. Consider it a holiday from your life. I know without a doubt, that you will adjust just fine."

Etta did not answer him. She hung her head, picking at her fingers, focusing on her hands in her lap.

Most girls weren't pleased when they first arrived, but Etta had signed the contract and willingly agreed to join the establishment that Philip had created. He hoped she would not take the typical step backward, resulting in her being given enemas and bare bottom spankings due to her lack of discipline. He had seen it time and time again with the new girls. By telling her what to expect, he was trying to save her the pain that would follow later. Etta seemed to be a good girl, and with the proper upbringing, she would please her papa.

He had felt the urge earlier at dinner, and it was now growing stronger by the minute; Philip realized he wanted to be that Papa. Yes, it was his desire for this pretty little blonde before him to be schooled properly to be *his* little love.

When he had created the chateau, after his wife's death, he had promised himself he would never fall for any of the little ones. They were to be married off to men who wielded power and desired full submission. He had met many of these men in his role as a lawyer, which was what kept him from giving up the practice entirely. It gave him access to the world of dominants in search for a young woman to satisfy their hidden cravings. Most had money and power, and could easily have any young woman of status that they wished, her dowry meaning very little. But men like this were particular and aggressive, which meant they only wanted the best—and Etta had potential to be the very best.

But Philip wanted Etta as his own little one. Was that such a terrible proposition to make? He had earned his own happiness, with all he had done for others. Staring at her, with her tiny little hands nervously folded on her lap like a good little girl, he knew she could give that to him, if he allowed her.

"Would you be willing to call me 'Papa', little Etta?" Philip leaned forward, his knees brushing against hers.

"I do not understand," she whispered.

"You will, love. You will."

She glanced up from her lap to meet his eyes. Fear was evident in her features. He had scared her. That had not been his intention, not in the slightest.

Philip changed seats, climbing across the small carriage to sit beside her. He wrapped his arm around her shoulders. "You're freezing," he said, acknowledging the shiver coursing through her body. Had it been the cold, or her nerves? His arm grazed her shoulders, and he felt her stiffen. The cloak around her body felt cool.

"I shall be fine," she said, but made no attempt to push him away.

"We have a long ride ahead of us, and the night air is only going to grow chillier. We might as well rest." He shut his eyes, pretending to sleep. Philip was not tired, in fact, he felt alive and more awake than he had in months, if not years. His heart had found its way back to him; beating soundly and with a steady rhythm.

Etta seemed to understand his intent and allowed her eyes to flutter closed, resting her head on his shoulder. It was exactly as he wished. He wrapped his arms around her, cuddling her as he would a child. Philip listened to the steady sound of her breathing as she drifted off to sleep. He hoped she would not be the typical handful he expected with new littles when they arrived at the chateau, but he could not be certain until morning came.

Hours passed, and she'd shifted slightly but had not stirred herself awake. Upon their arrival, Philip carried her from the coach and inside to her bedroom. He laid her atop the mattress and gestured for Nanny Mae to come into her room to finish tucking little Etta into bed.

Philip backed out of the room and shut the door, already missing her warm breath against his neck and her body curled into his. He hoped the next day would go just as smoothly, but something told him that her fears and the sadness she had experienced would not simply go away. Her memories and pain... it would take time to recover from such a devastating loss.

He knew about loss. His wife had died five years previously, and it had taken him time to heal. That had been when he'd made the chateau his passion, creating the establishment and opening it up to the right clientele. Not everyone could join or participate, even if they did have a wealth of cash. Philip had been particular to make sure that the papas all had strong morals and good intentions. His littles wouldn't be given to just any man. The right little, the right man, and the right circumstances were crucial, and his steadfast and dedication were the reasons why Ashby Chateau was becoming so successful.

FIVE

ETTA ROLLED over on the warm plush mattress, feeling the blankets cocooning her. Morning sun streamed in through the sheer white curtains, forcing her to wake far too early for her liking. What time was it?

Her eyes searched the unfamiliar room and as she sat up in bed, the sheets fell to her waist. Someone had changed her clothes! Had Philip been the one to undress her? Her stomach flopped at the thought that he might have seen her naked.

Anger bubbled within in her veins as her nostrils flared and she exhaled a heavy breath.

"Little Etta, you are awake," a red-haired, fair-skinned woman said. She had the most alluring blue eyes Etta had ever seen, with flecks of emerald green that made it impossible not to stare. There was an innocence behind her eyes, as well as a warm inviting smile. Freckles covered her nose and cheeks. Captivated by the young woman, Etta tried to understand why she was calling her 'little'. She hadn't been little since she was a child. Had the woman lost her mind? "I am Nanny Mae," the woman went on. "If you need anything, you ask me. All right?"

Etta felt confident that the woman must have banged her head. She didn't need a nanny—and certainly not a woman who barely had any more life experience than she had. If anyone was to be considered a child, this woman had the features more closely matched to a young one than she did; with a small button nose, thin lips, and tiny ears.

"Who undressed me?" Etta asked, staring down at the transparent pink gown. Her nipples were visible through the material, as was her pubic hair. In haste, she closed her legs and pulled the covers back up around her body to shield herself from being indecent.

"I did, of course." Nanny Mae reached for Etta, pulling her from the bed and onto the floor. "You were too asleep to even help me last night. Your papa brought you in far past your bedtime. Do you need to use the potty, little one?"

"I am not little," Etta said, stomping her foot. Why would this woman consider it proper to call her so? It infuriated her to no end. Had Philip thought so little of Etta that he felt she belonged in a nursery? Pale pink walls enclosed the room. A border of hand-painted blue and purple flowers with ivy skirted the edge of the ceiling around the room. A single window admitted the morning light, covered with sheer fabric that was dyed in a mix of blues, pinks, and purple that matched the overall décor.

Nanny Mae grabbed Etta by the arm and dragged her to a potty that was nestled in the corner of the nursery. "Sit!"

Etta made a face, displeased, but needing to use the chamber pot all the same. "Do you have to watch?" She found it embarrassing and absolutely improper to have Nanny Mae standing over her. Not even her own father had watched her use the chamber pot.

She was a grown woman. Why didn't the red-head recognize that?

"I have seen it all before. Do not be shy. Now hurry up and go potty like a good little girl."

Not being able to hold back her need any longer, Etta finished her business as fast as she could, glaring at the woman in front of her. Nanny Mae grabbed a cloth, moved quickly toward Etta's exposed cunny and, without hesitation, wiped between her legs.

"I can do that myself!" Etta ripped the cloth from her fingers and, in the process, knocked over the chamber pot.

"Etta!" Nanny Mae shook her head. "Come with me, right this instant."

She dragged Etta by the arm back to the bed, her grip pressing firmly, and sat her on the edge of the bed. Within seconds, the nanny had hoisted Etta over her lap and lifted her gown, revealing her bare bottom. The indecency of having no undergarments shot a humiliating heat straight to Etta's face.

Etta did not know what to expect, but it could not be good. "Oh, madam! You cannot!"

"I most certainly can, and I will, my dear." Mae swatted her bottom hard on each upturned cheek. "This is not how I wanted us to first be acquainted, but I do have a duty to uphold. I cannot have a charge of mine act in such naughty ways!"

Nanny Mae spanked Etta hard on her bottom again, repeating the horrid action over and over. Etta whimpered in pain, clenching her cheeks together. Tears formed at the corners of her eyes as her bottom ignited in a stinging heat. Etta could not recall the last time she had been corrected by someone else. It was quite possible she had never been spanked before. She certainly couldn't remember anything as dreadful as this. But to be spanked as an adult—the humiliation was almost too much to bear.

Over and over, Nanny Mae's hand peppered her behind. Her firm hand left no skin untouched as the spanking continued.

"Please, no," Etta said, in between pleas to be set free. "I shall clean up the mess. I won't do it again!" She was not even sure what she had done wrong. She had only wanted to clean herself after using the chamber pot, and the ensuing mess had been an accident. What was so terrible about that? "Madam, please!"

Mae swatted her even harder, in the spot where her thigh met the curve of her ass, causing Etta to yelp out in pain. "You will address me as Nanny Mae. Are we clear?"

Swat after swat continued in that most dreadful spot. No matter how much Etta wiggled to avoid the stinging blows, Nanny Mae always met her target with painful accuracy. "Yes, Nanny Mae. Yes!" Etta cried.

"You will learn to listen to me, or I shall be forced to tell Papa Philip what a bad little girl you were. Do you want me to do that?"

Philip did not seem to be an overly cruel or strict man, but then again, Etta barely knew him. The best course of action was to behave. "Please don't tell him." In truth, a small part of her was curious about what he'd do should he discover her naughty behavior. She did not mind the thought of him taking her over his knee if he was the one doing the disciplining. Anything would be better than her precarious situation at the moment.

Nanny Mae had a firm hand for such a small woman. She could not have been much older than Etta. In another life, perhaps they could have been sisters. Nanny Mae kept paddling Etta's bottom, reddening the milky-white flesh until Etta was convinced it would be difficult to sit for at least the rest of the morning.

"I asked you a question," Nanny Mae said, giving Etta another smack.

"I shall behave!" Etta cried out, her hips bucking with each swat as she tried to escape the torture, but Nanny Mae would not let her go.

Four more swats, and tears were flowing down her cheeks freely like the Thames.

"I think you've had enough and have learned your lesson." Nanny Mae placed Etta's feet back on the floor, her nightgown falling past her waist. "Remember, child, there are worse punishments than spankings for bad behavior at the chateau."

Etta's eyes widened and she took a step back, covering her backside in case the nanny changed her mind about being finished.

"Go and sit on your bed quietly while I clean up the floor."

Whimpering, Etta backed up toward the bed, glancing at it and then to Nanny Mae. She was not keen on sitting on her sore bottom, her skin being raw, but she did not dare risk angering Nanny Mae further. If she did not listen to this woman, would she find her bottom in far worse condition? The nanny had threatened her about worse punishments —what could they possibly be? What could be worse and more humiliating for a grown woman than being spanked like an errant child?

Etta climbed onto the bed and lay on her stomach. She propped her head up on her hands and stared at Nanny Mae as she mopped up the mess that had been made. Watching with fascination, she wondered what other tasks the nanny was responsible for. She had never known anyone to clean up after her when she had knocked something over—well, at least not since childhood. Even stranger was the fact that it was a disgusting chamber pot.

The pain of her sore bottom faded to a tingle as she watched Nanny Mae cleaning the oak floor, cursing under her breath. When the woman had completed her task, she stood up and adjusted her attire, pressing the loose curls that had escaped the pins in her hair back into place. With a straightening of her spine and a slight huff of breath, Nanny Mae once again resembled the proper and firm governess.

"Come here for your bath, little one."

As if on cue, another young woman carried buckets of hot water into the room, pouring them into a porcelain bathtub in the corner. Etta knew what was next, even before hearing Nanny Mae's shout for her to come and be washed. With reluctance, she climbed off the mattress and walked toward Nanny Mae, as slowly as possible.

"Hands up. We have to take off that night gown," the nanny said.

"I do not want you to watch me take a bath." Etta was not pleased with the arrangement. Why was this woman looking after her? Where was Philip? Though she would not have felt comfortable with him watching her bathe either, there was still something deep inside her that wanted him nearby.

"Little girls do not take baths by themselves. Arms up!"

Etta crossed her arms over her chest, making it difficult—though not impossible—for Nanny Mae to undress her easily. The nanny swatted her throbbing bottom, spanking her once, then twice. Long enough for Etta's arms to drop and cover her rear.

In one swift motion, Nanny Mae lifted the gown up over Etta's head and arms, leaving her standing completely naked.

Etta covered her intimate areas with her arms.

"Do not be so prudish, child," the nanny said, tsking under her breath. She checked the water temperature. "It is still slightly warm. Why don't we get you prepared first, then bathe you after we are done?"

"Prepared? After what?" Etta asked. What was this woman talking about?

The nanny disappeared out of the room and came back moments later with a few towels, a straight razor, and a bar of shaving soap.

Etta's heart skipped a beat. "What do you plan on doing with that?"

"Littles do not have any hair on their pretty pink cunnies. Papa wants me to shave it all off. Will you be a good girl, or do I need to ask the other papas to come in and hold you down, child?"

Etta slowly backed away from Nanny Mae. The thought of the nanny nicking her folds scared her more than anything else had so far that morning. "What if you cut me?"

"I have not cut a little in four years—well, not unless they moved and fought me the entire time," the nanny said.

Etta was not pleased with the situation. She glanced from the straight razor to the door. How far could she get? At the moment, she was naked, and the nightgown was far too inadequate to snatch and take with her if she ran. Besides, she had no money and no home. She did not even know where the chateau was located, and her uncle would not be pleased upon her return. The young woman felt trapped in a life she did not want.

"I will not ask you again."

Etta swallowed nervously. "I shall be a good girl." Her heart slammed against her chest, the beating of her heart echoing through her ears. Didn't Nanny Mae hear it too?

"Come with me," Nanny Mae said, placing a towel on the mattress. "I want you to lie down at the edge of the bed and spread your legs."

Etta made no attempt to move.

The nanny swatted her bottom and Etta jumped, climbing atop the mattress, lying back on the fresh clean towel.

"I said spread your legs." Nanny Mae guided Etta's thighs apart as she bent down and lathered the shaving soap all over her folds. "Vivian! Bring me a tub of warm water!" she commanded.

The same young woman with dark black hair who had been filling the bathtub poked her head into the bedroom. "Yes, of course, Nanny Mae." She reappeared a few minutes later bringing a sloshing bowl of water to the room.

Mae placed it on the bed and then glanced at Etta. "Be careful, little girl. You do not want to get burned."

Etta did not say a word. She lay there, practically holding her breath as the nanny dipped the razor in the warm water before dragging it slowly down between her thighs over the long, coarse blonde hair. Mae rinsed the hair and soap away before making a second stroke, her finger spreading apart Etta's folds to better see what she was doing. With caution, she worked on the outer folds first before making sure all the fuzz was long gone from Etta's most intimate region.

The young woman remained silent, afraid to move, fearful that Nanny Mae might just cut her out of spite for her actions. It was not as though Etta had been a model new student at the school. She'd ended up making the nanny clean the contents of the piss pot from the floor. If the tables were turned, it would certainly cross Etta's mind.

She shut her eyes and clenched the bed sheets, afraid to watch, not that she could see what was happening until it was done. Her position was unflattering at best.

The door opened and Philip locked eyes with Etta.

She wanted to slam her legs shut and deny him the sight of her naked body, but she felt the razor stroking down, coming right alongside her clit. There was no way she was going to move and risk injury. A flush spread from her cheeks... down her neck and across her breasts.

Philip did well not to stare at her naked form, his eyes remained on her face the entire time. How did he manage to do that? It must have taken great restraint.

"I hope you are doing well this morning," he said as he approached Nanny Mae and stood beside her, looking down at her progress with the cunny shaving. "How has she been, Nanny Mae?"

The woman cleared her throat and met Etta's blue stare. "Nothing I could not handle, for a new pupil."

Why had Nanny Mae lied for Etta? Had she been concerned about him finding out the truth, that she could not be controlled, or was the nanny doing her a favor, trying to help her out? Etta watched their exchange, not saying a word.

"I am pleased to hear it," Philip said and nodded, seeming gratified with the news.

He ran his finger along the cleanly shaven flesh, checking the nanny's handiwork. Etta gasped, but remained still, since the razor still rested precariously close to her clit.

His finger ran from the top of her pussy lip all the way to her taint, pausing right before making contact with her anus. He reached out with his other hand, gently took the razor out of Nanny Mae's hand and began stroking it along Etta's skin, finishing Nanny Mae's job for her.

The man was shaving her private bits and she could do nothing about it. She couldn't even find the words to plead, or demand, or even ask nicely for him to stop. A tingling sensation attacked her cunny, and her little pearl throbbed in need. Philip's fingers maneuvered her flesh around so he could shave the remaining hair, every ministration somehow enhancing her need for more. His touch... the way he studied her bare cunny... the way she was lying with her legs spread wide before him... the way she remained helpless at his hand, and not wanting to fight the act in the slightest.

"Very nice, Nanny Mae. Very nice indeed." He pulled his hand away, handing the razor back to the nanny, and made his way back to the door. "After her morning bath, I would like to have her join me for breakfast. Do you think you can make that happen?"

"Yes, sir. Of course," Mae said.

Did the nanny ever tell him no? If she was not mistaken, Philip Hartley was the nanny's employer. Etta doubted that Nanny Mae would not have tried to make Etta ready on time, even if it was an impossibility. She'd probably send her to visit him naked if they ran out of time.

"I shall see you later, my little one." He gave a brief wave and left her bedroom, closing the door behind him.

Etta breathed a sigh of relief once he left the two of them alone.

"That was not so bad," Nanny Mae said, finished with the razor. "You are smooth now, just as Papa Philip likes it. Do you know you are the first girl who is here just for him?"

Etta did not quite know what that meant, but she suspected it was a good thing. "Oh?" she asked.

"Come now. It is time for your bath. You will not have time to play. We need to get you washed and dressed so that Papa can see you again for breakfast."

SIX

IT HAD TAKEN Philip all the restraint in the world not to claim little Etta right then and there as he had stared down at her beautiful blossoming body, drinking in the sight of her perky breasts and the half-shaven hair that Nanny Mae had worked to remove. He had never shaved a little before, but found the chore quite delightful.

His cock throbbed in his pants as he walked back to his room.

He had made all the papas wait until the girls had graduated before they could have their way with the ladies. He would not allow himself to break his own rules, just so he could fuck her tight little quim.

Philip needed a distraction. Just knowing that Etta would be going for her bath was making his cock rock solid in his trousers. He stalked down the stark white hall, heading for the playroom in order to check on the other littles and their papas. The ceiling looked like the outside sky, for it had been painted in a pale blue with wisps of white clouds, as it would be on a sunny day. The curtains covering the windows matched the walls with a warm, sunny yellow. When Philip had helped in designing the layout of the nursery, he had insisted on replicating as much of an outdoor feeling as possible, since the littles were to be kept mostly indoors.

Shelves of toys lined the furthest wall from the door, with everything from blocks to stuffed animals. Philip had hired the best doll makers and craftsmen, insisting that the toys were to be gifts. Very few could know the truth without repercussions.

Near the door, a white-painted wooden table was most often used for the nannies to sit at and speak to one another, or for the papas to discuss their little ones with one another. At the opposite wall by the door, a rocking chair had seen more use than most of the items in the nursery. The worn wood needed a good refinishing, but a replacement hadn't yet been purchased, and to go without a rocking chair for any length of time would prove difficult.

Papa Francis, a banker with whom Philip had done quite a lot of business, sat in the rocking chair, cuddling Leda. Her nanny had dressed her in a dark red gown with a bright white bow on the front. She wore a bonnet, and her cheeks were as red as the dress, which served only to make her look far younger. Had her papa been giving her special attention? Papa Francis's daily time with Leda was limited, what with his job and, more importantly, the visiting hours the chateau allowed for the papas. The little ones were on a strict schedule to instill discipline, which meant the papas could not break the rules either. Leda's brown unruly curls had been tamed, much like the young woman. On her arrival she'd been bossy and bratty, disinterested in following the rules, and the staff had soon found that a harsh spanking had not been enough to keep the girl in line. Leda had had her bottom bruised on more than one occasion as she displayed poor choices repeatedly.

At the moment, she sat curled in her papa's embrace, his hands smoothing over her back as he cuddled the little one in his arms.

"Leda," Philip said, coming toward the rocking chair. He bent down, drawing closer to her eye level. "I want you to be a good girl and show our newest little Etta the playroom. Will you do that after she has finished with her bath?"

The young brunette was a few years older than Etta. She had been at the Ashby Chateau far longer than any other student. Her Papa Francis had paid a great deal to ensure her submission to him, but it had not come as easily as any of the staff would have liked. Leda had been temperamental, insubordinate, and had even run away on two separate occasions.

Philip was taking a huge risk by asking his most troublesome pupil to help guide Etta to be a good little one. He had to trust that the work he'd done with Leda would last, and that she'd seen the error of her ways and would not make the same mistakes a fourth time around.

Leda nodded, staring up at her papa. "I shall show her the new dollhouse. We can play with it together."

"That would be nice of you, child." Philip stood back up. "Why don't you go and play so your papa and I can have a word alone?"

The brunette clung to her papa, unwilling to let him go.

"Leda," Papa Francis's voice was stern, "you need to listen to Headmaster Philip."

Whining, she untangled herself from her papa's embrace and sauntered off toward the oversized dollhouse that had been made especially for the little ones.

Philip waited until Leda was out of earshot. "I have been wanting to discuss with you Leda's progress. I think it is time we considered finishing her schooling here and sending her home to live with you."

Francis frowned.

The joyous look that Philip had expected on the papa's face never came. "Is there something wrong, Francis?"

"I have some concerns that Leda's submission is an act so she can finish with the chateau and leave the facility."

Philip's brow furrowed and his expression turned grim. "Do you have any proof of this game you believe her to be playing?"

Francis shook his head. "She has done everything asked of her in the past six months. We have connected physically and emotionally, but something does not feel quite right."

Philip expelled a heavy sigh. "Perhaps it is merely because you are used to Leda's temper and insubordination. Do you prefer her unruly behavior?" Philip had seen it before, the papas becoming attached to the discipline more than the reward-seeking behavior. Some men found their sexual appetite wetted with harsh spankings, and as their little began to behave, their desire diminished. Philip had worked diligently to weed out such cases, undertaking a thorough examination of each papa before admitting their little into his school.

Francis watched Leda from across the room as she played with her doll and the dollhouse. "No. I do not believe that is the case. I truly feel that her behavior will change when we leave together."

Philip understood how Francis felt. "There will be an adjustment the first few days, and that is why we can send a nanny to accompany you to ensure Leda has adjusted appropriately. Of course, there will be an additional charge for those services."

"Paying you is not the problem. I am concerned Leda will leave me, Philip. Her desire is shown, but I do not always feel it."

"We shall keep you both at Ashby for a little while longer. When you are ready to take Leda home, I shall make sure Nanny Mae or another nanny can accompany you both home. I assure you, Francis, you will not be disappointed."

"Thank you."

Philip left the playroom, his stomach tense. Had he made a mistake deciding to put Leda and Etta together? If Leda had been fooling the system, then surely she'd teach Etta the same tricks. No. Francis had to be paranoid. Philip had never known a little one to be so manipulative after spending five years at the chateau. His own, new little one would be just fine.

SEVEN

ETTA CLIMBED INTO THE BATHTUB. The water was warm but not as steaming as she'd have liked it. Her fingers moved along the surface, making slight waves with a back and forth motion. She did not try and fight Nanny Mae, as it did very little good. Her bottom felt sore, especially in the warm water, and she did not dare risk another swat.

Nanny Mae grabbed a small cloth and dunked it in to wet it. She reached for the bar of soap, creating enough suds to get Etta clean. The woman ran the cloth over and down her back, paying attention to every inch of her bare skin. No one had ever been so attentive to Etta before; it felt strange, yet satisfying.

"Your papa will be so proud of you, child." Nanny Mae washed Etta's back and arms, then moved the cloth around to the young woman's chest, soaping up her breasts and down between her thighs where she'd just been shaven.

Etta relaxed under the woman's touch and as her fingers caressed the silky folds of her quim, she realized that she wanted Nanny Mae to touch her more than just a quick swipe. She shifted in the bath, desperately trying to find the woman's fingers as the nanny's hand moved the cloth to her legs and then down each muscular calf.

"Sit still. You are getting water everywhere."

Etta stopped moving, the cloth being too far from her desired area for it to do any good. Would the woman scold her if she touched herself in the bath? She was not sure she had the nerve to do it, and yet her sex pulsed beneath her, begging to be satisfied. So wanton, so improper, so... All proper decorum and etiquette had vanquished the moment she had let a man shave the curls from her privates. Not caring anymore about how a lady would act, Etta's hand snaked down into the water, caressing her bare pussy.

The moment she touched her clit, Nanny Mae swatted her hands away and pinched her nipple, causing both a yelp of arousal and a whine from the unpleasant jolt of pain coursing through her body. She let go as fast as she'd done the action. "Good little girls do not touch themselves. They let their papa please them. Do that again and I shall be forced to tell Papa Philip how naughty you are and how you have disappointed him," Mae scolded her.

Etta shook her head. Philip had been kind to her. She did not want to upset him, unsure as she was as to what the consequences would be. Already she had endured enough of a rough spanking to know that it would not be pleasant to have another one.

Nanny Mae clasped the wet cloth and roughly washed over Etta's sensitive bottom.

Whining, Etta thrashed in the water, trying to escape nanny's harsh touch against her freshly marked rear.

"Hold still, child." Nanny Mae smacked Etta's clenched cheeks.

The sting hurt far worse than the earlier ones she'd been given. Was it the warm water that caused the burn to spread, or the fact that she already had raw skin that did not desire another swat?

With no way to escape the clutches of Nanny Mae, Etta held still a moment longer, the bath nearly being done.

"Stand up." Nanny Mae ordered Etta to her feet and grabbed a white towel, wrapping it around her petite frame. She rubbed the linen between her folds, patting her cunny dry, and every inch of skin, leaving her hair in wet tangles. Then the nanny grabbed a second towel, twirling Etta's long blonde locks into it, twisting it up and securing it on her head.

Dry and chilly from the cool air in the room, Etta allowed Nanny Mae to escort her into the bedroom, where she opened the wooden armoire, revealing an array of brightly colored dresses. She removed one that was navy blue with white highlights. It was a little girl's sailor dress. Nanny Mae grabbed a pair of little white bloomers with frills around the edges that would rest just below Etta's bum. This was not the attire of a proper young lady—it was quite scandalous, in fact.

"Is there anything else in there?" Etta asked. In addition to scandalous, the dress looked rather childish.

"Your papa made a special request to see you in this dress for breakfast. Arms up," Nanny Mae said, with a strict tone that meant business. Etta lifted her arms above her head, letting her nanny slide the gown over her head and her arms through the sleeves. "Turn around, child."

Etta turned around and Nanny Mae laced up the back of the gown before reaching for the white bloomers, helping Etta into the white cotton one leg at a time.

They were huge and unattractive, sticking out from below the hem as the sailor dress was much too short, even for her. Etta was not incredibly tall, and she certainly was nowhere near Nanny Mae's height or her papa's stature.

"Sit on the bed," Nanny Mae said, instructing her for the final preparations. She helped guide the white stockings up Etta's legs. They came to her thighs, with little dark blue and white striped bows affixed to the top. Mae then removed a pair of shiny black shoes and slipped them on to Etta's feet, securing the straps through the buckles.

Etta did not dare ask how she looked. She felt ridiculous, but Nanny Mae smiled as though she were proud of her accomplishment.

The nanny returned to the washroom, finding a hairbrush and two bands. She untangled Etta's blonde tresses, splitting her hair in two sections from the middle and plaiting both sides.

Etta made faces as her nanny tugged on the roots of her hair. It was uncomfortable feeling the pull against her scalp and the tightening of each strand as it was cinched together to make it look beautiful.

She wished there'd been a mirror in the room, for her to see her reflection. If there had been, she'd probably laugh at how foolish she looked. Did Philip desire this to make a mockery of her? How was this a proper education for marriage?

"Come, child. It is time I take you to your papa and you share a meal together." Nanny Mae held out her hand and Etta took it, climbing down from the bed as she followed her out of the room and down the hall.

It was the first Etta had seen of the school aside from her nursery. The pale white walls seemed to stretch on forever, with closed doors at every juncture.

"Does Philip live here, at the school?" Etta asked.

Nanny Mae dropped the young woman's hand and smacked her clothed bottom. "You must refer to Headmaster Philip as 'Papa'. Is that clear?"

Etta swallowed anxiously and nodded with vigor. "Yes, of course." She understood that if she did not please her nanny and probably Philip, her papa, then there'd be consequences. Her bottom could not take any further abuse today.

As they stepped from the hall into the dining room, Etta's black shoes clicked across the floor. She glanced down at the sound, curious to know whether she would leave scuff marks if she weren't so careful. Would she find herself punished for that behavior as well? Her feet dragged slightly as she walked, testing her shoes. Sure enough, black strokes glazed the marble floor.

"Pick your feet up, child!" Nanny Mae scolded her.

Etta walked the correct way, until she found herself standing in front of her papa. It felt strange to call him such a name.

"Have a seat, little one." Papa pulled out the chair, helping guide her closer to the table once she sat down. He handed her a napkin. "Place this on your lap, so you do not mess up that pretty dress of yours."

Etta took the black cloth napkin and set it across her lap over the dress. She did not care if she soiled the garment, but she suspected Nanny Mae would not be pleased with her.

Nanny Mae left the two of them alone. Etta breathed a sigh of relief. Perhaps she could voice her questions to Philip. Now that it was just the two of them, hopefully he'd find it in his heart to answer her concerns. "I do not understand why I am here," Etta said. She got right to the point. She knew enough about Philip to understand he'd done well for himself. This was his school and his pride. She did not wish in any way to offend him.

"Your uncle wanted me to look after you. Do you not recall the conversation from the other night?" His brow furrowed.

"I do," Etta said. She even remembered the contract she'd signed, though the language had been complicated and intense. Honestly, she did not know what she had agreed to, other than to go with him. Slowly, she was beginning to see the error she'd made. "You do realize I am twenty, Mr. Hartley. Look at me!" She gestured to the sailor's outfit. It was ridiculous. Even a young child would look silly—but a grown woman... it felt absurd to be wearing such an item.

"You will address me as 'Papa', and you look very nice, Etta."

She did not feel that way. Uncomfortable was only the beginning to explain the mix of emotions coursing through her veins. "I thought your chateau was a finishing school," she said. "I was under the impression that I would learn to be a lady, so that I might find a suitable husband to marry." Philip had sworn to her uncle that he'd marry her off, but she was not in agreement with either of their way of thinking.

"Yes, we do have some students in the eastern wing who are strictly here for finishing school. You, my child, are here for something greater, a special purpose that is selected for only the best, most talented and gifted young women."

Etta blushed at his compliments. It was rare for anyone to be so flattering or kind to her.

"My school of littles is kept a secret from the finishing school to help quash any suspicions that might be cast upon someone entering the chateau. I have worked diligently to ensure the protection and anonymity of the men who join us for our exclusive school. We do not wish to soil anyone's reputation here."

Etta challenged him in every way possible. "Why do they need to keep what they are doing, what *you* are doing, a secret?"

Philip's eyes narrowed. "That is enough, Etta. I do not care for your tone." The conversation was over, and just in time, as breakfast was brought to the table. "Eat your eggs." He stood, moving closer toward her at the table.

With fork in hand, she nibbled on the scrambled eggs. They were seasoned and spicy, making her mouth water as she gobbled up as much food as she could. Her mouth hung agape as she stared up at him. Was he coming over to spank her?

He reached for his knife and grabbed her extra fork, cutting the sausage into small, bite-sized pieces.

She paused, stabbing her fork into one of the small pieces of sausage. She held it in the air as she spoke. "Why are you cutting up my food?"

Philip nodded toward the utensil in her hand. "Put that down when you speak. It is impolite to toss food around."

Sheepishly she placed the fork on her plate. She asked the question again. "Why do I not get a knife?" Did he think she'd use it as a weapon? She was not exactly being kept against her will, but she did not know what was being required of her at the time she signed the contract, either. Though, in truth, Etta had nowhere else to go, no trade, no job, or prospects of a husband.

"At the Ashbury Chateau, you are a little one. Everything will be provided for you. You need not have a care in the world, my little love. Do you remember when I told you it would be like going on holiday?"

"Yes."

"Was I wrong?" Philip asked.

It did not feel like a second home, or a trip to the ocean with the waves crashing on her feet and the sand sticking in her toes. However, she also felt free. In a way, he was right, and Etta hated to admit it, especially aloud. For years she'd spent her days caring for a dying man. Now she had someone who was interested in caring for her. She did not feel like she belonged though, did he not see that?

"I do not know how you want me to be," Etta said, her voice whiny. If she was supposed to please him, she was at a loss as to how.

"Just be yourself," Philip said. He kissed her forehead and sat back down at the table. "Now finish your breakfast, and if you are a good girl, you can go play in the playroom when you are done."

EIGHT

THE QUESTIONS WERE TIRESOME. Philip wanted to take Etta over his knee just to silence her, but he vowed only to use strict discipline when it was necessary. Her inquisitive mind was exactly like that of a child; questioning and curious over everything. He could not fault her for that.

Once they had finished breakfast, Philip had Nanny Mae take Etta to the playroom to meet the other littles.

His stomach gurgled at the thought of Etta and Leda plotting their escape from the chateau together. No. Leda was a good little one. Etta would take some time to accept her role as submissive, and there was no reason to believe otherwise.

He pushed all thoughts aside and stood, walking from the dining room out into the hall. The school was quiet, exceptionally so for an afternoon when classes were in session, though he knew the girls were busy in their classes, learning proper etiquette and behavior. Their afternoon break was often met with rowdiness and unruly young girls who needed a reminder to their bottoms about the proper way to behave.

Perhaps he should have gone to the eastern wing to check on the other girls, but he felt drawn toward the playroom. He wanted to watch Etta and see how she interacted with the other littles.

The wall between the playroom and the hall was made of glass, allowing him the opportunity to see his precious Etta. She seemed to pay no attention to him as he watched her.

Etta sat across from Leda and they appeared to be quietly chatting, each holding a doll and brushing her hair.

Philip had not learned to read lips, and was terrible at even attempting to try and make out what was being said. He stood for several minutes, watching the calm exchange between the two girls. They at least seemed to be getting along well enough.

"Headmaster Philip," Papa Lawrence said, stalking down the hall, his Gracie's hand nestled tight in his own.

"Yes, Lawrence." Philip clasped his hands together in front of him. "What can I do for you?"

Lawrence let go of the young blonde's hand. Though she and Etta were both blonde, Gracie's hair was mixed with highlights of red and gold, probably from her time in the sun. She'd been given special privileges to visit the outside gardens with her papa. Lawrence stared at Gracie and nodded. "Tell Headmaster Philip what you said to me about Leda."

Gracie's eyes widened and she shook her head, vigorously.

"Gracie." Lawrence's tone grew in intensity as he seemed to grow irritated by her behavior. He swatted her bottom. "Tell him what you said to me."

Her bottom lip trembled and her hands shook. "I do not want to."

Philip cleared his throat and motioned for Lawrence to leave the two of them alone. Philip guided Gracie toward his office and sat her down on the upholstered armchair. "Tell me what's going on, child."

"She is going to be mad at me."

"Not as mad as your papa. He's standing outside that door, waiting for you to enlighten me about what's going on."

"It is Leda," Gracie said, her voice hardly above a whisper. "She has been telling me how she does not really submit to her papa, she just lets him believe that so she can get out of here."

Philip did not typically like the girls tattling on one another, but in this instance, it was useful information that he needed to know. "Lawrence," he said, calling Gracie's papa back into the room.

"I would like you to give your little Gracie a special treat for being such a good girl and helping me out. Can you do that?" Philip asked. He knew Lawrence would be proud to have some alone time with his little one.

Lawrence took Gracie's hand and led her out of Philip's office.

Philip rubbed his forehead, frustrated. It seemed as though Francis had not been imagining the scenario that Leda was fooling them. Now it was up to him as headmaster to devise a plan to ensure she'd learn her lesson and keep the other girls in line. The only problem was figuring out what would work. Everything he had done to force her to submit had been beneficial in the moment but had not offered the long-term effects he'd anticipated.

Stepping out from his office, he roamed the halls, finding the dark-haired maid mopping the floor. "Vivian, can I have a word with you?"

Vivian had always assisted Nanny Mae, but she'd never been tasked to instill discipline in any of the littles. She was allowed to dish out a punishment, as all adults at the school were, but she had never felt the need—or perhaps the desire. Philip was not sure which.

He needed her to step up and take a stronger role with the littles.

"Yes, of course." Vivian placed the mop against the wall and followed Philip to his office.

He shut the door behind him. "Have a seat," he said, gesturing to the chair that had just a few minutes earlier seated Gracie.

Vivian took a seat, her hands on the armrests. "Have I done something wrong, Mr. Hartley?"

Philip shook his head. "No. I would like to hire a second nanny, and I thought that you might be interested in the position. It is certainly a step up from being a maid at our school."

Her beautiful brown eyes glistened with tears. Was she excited about the promotion, or frightened of what it meant she'd be doing? "I would like that very much," she said.

"Good. I need you to start right away. Our little Leda is not being the precious girl she is pretending to be. Have you heard anything about this?" Philip was curious to know if other staff members were aware of her insubordination but choosing to keep their heads down.

"Leda's always had a difficult time adjusting to the submissive lifestyle," Vivian answered. She may not have been a nanny, but Philip suspected that she witnessed everything at the school.

"I have two sources telling me that she may not really be submitting to her papa as she is leading everyone to believe," Philip said. He was not going to give away his two sources, in case Vivian slipped up. She may have spent time around the girls, but disciplining them was an entirely different course of action. Would she have it in her to follow the rules of the school? It was not for everyone, and he would have to keep a close eye on her to make sure she did as instructed.

Vivian's lips pursed together. "How would you like me to proceed, sir?"

He made the rules of the institution; it was the nannies who instilled them.

"You will keep a watchful eye over Leda. She is your responsibility, Vivian. Can you handle her?"

Philip was not really giving her much of a choice. Leda needed the undivided attention of one nanny, and he had to trust that Vivian was up to the task. If he was not busy keeping an eye on Etta, he would discipline the little himself and remind her who was in charge.

NINE

"I'M LEDA," the girl with dark brown hair said. Her hair was sectioned into two pigtails, just like Etta's. Leda was dressed in a blue and white gingham dress, with a petticoat sticking out from underneath to make her skirt fuller.

"Etta." She chewed her bottom lip, glancing back at her nanny by the door.

"Do not be scared of Nanny Mae. She is quite the pushover," Leda said. She kept her voice down. "Come here, I shall tell you everything you need to know about her to avoid getting spanked."

Etta's stomach bubbled as she followed the girl toward the dollhouse.

Leda handed her a doll. "Pretend we are playing."

"But we are playing, aren't we?" Etta asked, not understanding what Leda was up to.

"We just have to make it look like we are playing. The grownups do not pay that close attention to us," Leda said. She grabbed a hairbrush for her doll and worked the tangles from her hair. "I have been here for five years, Etta. If anyone knows what it takes to get out, I do."

Etta felt overwhelmed. "Five years?" She'd been under the impression that she would be at the school for a little while, but she did not think her time would last that long. "Why so long? Can they not find you someone to marry?"

"Marry?" Leda laughed and shook her head. "I am betrothed to Francis. He's my papa. Just as you are to marry your own papa someday."

"I am?" Etta asked. She knew her uncle wanted her to marry, and he had enrolled her in the school to better help her chances of finding a good husband. Her nanny had made mention of Philip taking a liking to her and no one else, though he had not come out and said that he was going to marry her. She groaned, feeling confused.

"Do you want to know the secret of getting out of here for good?" Leda asked.

Etta frowned, thoroughly confused. If she was going to marry Philip, then there was no true way of ever getting out. Didn't Leda see that, too, about her Papa Francis?

When Etta did not answer, the young brunette continued talking, while brushing her doll's hair. She focused on her toy, pretending to be enthralled with it. "The men expect us to submit to them in every way possible. Make them believe you do, and you will be set free."

"Free?" Etta did not find the chateau that bad a place. It was odd and strange for her, but she did not exactly want to leave.

"Yes. Once your papa sets you free and allows you to leave the Ashby Chateau, you will be able to escape his home. You do not really think that our papas live here all year round?"

"Don't they?" Etta asked. Her mind felt heavily fogged with all of Leda's thoughts. Why had her papa insisted they become friends? Did he know what Leda was up to? Had he intentionally been trying to give her a message as well; that if she behaved, then she, too, would be free of him and her uncle?

"No, silly," Leda said, shaking her head and laughing. "They visit on weekends and holidays. You are lucky. Your papa works here. You will probably see him every day."

Seeing Philip every day did not sound so terrible. Why was Leda making all of this out to be one horrible scenario? Her papa had been good to her. Though it did feel strange to be dressed in children's clothes and referring to Philip as Papa, Etta could manage it if it meant she were content. Right now, aside from a slightly sore bottom, she was happier than she had been in a long time.

The playroom door opened and Vivian, the young woman who had brought buckets of water for Etta's bath, entered into the room. She spoke briefly with Nanny Mae, forcing Etta's stomach to flip over. Was she in trouble?

"Leda, playtime is over," Vivian said.

Leda glanced up, dropping the doll to the floor. "You are not my nanny."

"Come, child, I do not have all day." Vivian reached for Leda's arm, dragging her from the playroom and out into the hall.

Etta watched with fascinated curiosity. Where was she heading?

Nanny Mae sauntered toward Etta. "Are you having fun?"

What constituted fun to Nanny Mae? Etta was sitting on the floor, brushing her doll's hair. Leda had scared Etta, talking such nonsense about pretending to be pleased. Feeling overwhelmed, Etta's eyes watered and her bottom lip trembled. She did not want to have to pretend. Etta wanted to be happy. She desired a papa who cared for her and looked after her. Didn't Leda's papa do that for her? Etta hung her head as tears dripped onto the carpet.

"Little one, what is it?" Nanny Mae asked, drawing her finger under Etta's chin, lifting her head to meet her gaze. "Tell your nanny what is wrong."

"It is nothing." She sniffled, her eyes darting back down to the ground. Etta did not want to disappoint Papa or Nanny Mae.

"Did little Leda tell you a nasty tale?" Nanny Mae asked.

Etta cast her gaze back up toward her nanny. "She is not very nice." She worried about confessing what she'd heard and getting punished for it. What if they did not believe her? Leda had been there for years, and it was Etta's first day at the chateau.

Nanny Mae knelt down and wrapped her arms around Etta, kissing her softly on the forehead. "Do not cry. All will be fine." She took out a handkerchief and dried Etta's eyes. "Come, child, it is time for you to see the doctor."

"Doctor?" Etta was not sick. Why were they having her visit the doctor?

"Yes." Nanny Mae grabbed Etta's arm and hoisted her from the ground, leading her out into the hallway. "Doctor Colt is waiting for you. Do not be shy." She led Etta through the hall and toward a door that had been closed on the right. Without knocking, she opened it, whisking the little one inside, then closed the door—leaving Etta to stand in the room without her.

Etta swallowed nervously, staring at the examination table and black leather bag on a nearby desk. Both items stood out against the stark white walls of the room. Not a single painting had been hung or a dash of color had found the walls, except for the scuff where the door had banged the wall. The room smelled sterile and the scent burned her nose, forcing her to grimace as her nose wrinkled, trying to rid the scent from her nostrils. Although she had been forced into the room, she made no attempt to step any closer to the men.

Philip stood beside the gray-haired, crooked-nosed doctor, going over some notes. Phillip was a few inches taller than the plump man with the stethoscope. With Philip's broad shoulders and strong posture, Etta found it impossible to turn away. No doubt he was handsome, with his striking features, eyes as blue as the sea, and hair as thick and dark like the night, but there was something she found captivating in the way he spoke quietly, leaning in and tilting his head down slightly to speak to the doctor. It was the intimacy of the gesture, the desire she felt to be on the other end, to be given that type of attention. Were they talking about her? She had not seen a doctor in years, except when one had come to visit in regards to her father. Her own health seemed to be above average. She rarely got ill, but that had probably been because she was not ever in contact with anyone.

"Come inside, have a seat," Papa said. He patted the examination table.

Chewing her bottom lip nervously, Etta climbed atop the table, her legs dangling off. "Why am I here? I am not sick."

"Doctor Colt works with all the students at Ashby," Papa said. "His job is to make sure they are all in good health. He is going to do an examination on you today."

It was not a question. Etta did not seem to have a choice. "What kind of examination?" She remembered her father's doctor listening to his heart and ailing lungs.

"Doctor Colt is going to check your temperature, make sure your heart and lungs are strong, and that everything is working as it should be."

"All right." That did not sound so terrible.

"He is also going to examine you to make sure that your virginity is still intact."

Those words were enough encouragement to get Etta to bolt from the bed. "Mr. Hartley! I can assure you that is not necessary!"

"Papa," he warned, giving her a look that told her not to cross him. "And you, my little love, will do as I say."

"You mean he is going to look at me, down there?" Absolutely not. She had not agreed to anything of the sort. The very idea was humiliating and most scandalous!

"Not just look, child. We need to make sure that everything works as it should," Papa said. "I would hate to have to discipline you for misbehavior right here in front of Dr. Colt, so please be a good girl, and do as the doctor says."

Etta's heart felt as though it would beat outside of her chest. The small room was sweltering, and seeing as how it was situated in the middle of the chateau, there were no windows to let in any outside air. "It is hot in here." Her cheeks reddened and a sheen of sweat coated her skin from head to toe.

"Why don't you lie down?" Doctor Colt suggested, extending the table so Etta could put her feet on it as well.

"All right." With wide eyes, like that of a doe, she lay back, staring up at the ceiling. Her heart did not seem to be slowing but the nauseous pit in her stomach began to ease slightly, as did the intense heat from the room.

"I know you may be nervous, and that is perfectly natural. Just try and relax," Doctor Colt said. "We have all the time in the world, child."

She did not know if he was being condescending or if he was merely not in a rush with any other patients. As far as Etta knew, she was the newest and only student who had arrived within the last twenty-four hours.

Slowly her heart eased up and her nerves, though still unsettled, felt a bit better. Papa stood beside her, his hand gently rubbing her arm, coaxing her to submission. "That is a good girl," he said, soothing her. He leaned down and softly kissed her forehead. "I am proud of you, my little love."

"I am going to start with some simple tests, Etta. Do you think you can put this on for me?" It was an ugly piece of cloth that looked undoubtedly itchy. "I am going to step outside the room. Your papa is going to stay with you and help."

Was that one of the tests? Seeing if Etta could follow directions and change into the horrible gown? She did not answer the doctor.

He stepped out of the room and Papa glanced Etta over. "Are you going to obey, or do I need to call in Nanny Mae for help?"

Etta's eyes widened. She knew if he had to bring in Nanny Mae, then she'd probably get her bottom smacked again.

"I shall get changed."

"Good." Papa helped her down from the table and waited for her to disrobe as he held the gown in his hands.

"I need help with the dress. It is too tight to remove on my own."

"Oh." He nodded and placed the gown onto the table. "Put your arms up."

She did as instructed, and he reached down, lifting the dress up and over her head, helping her remove it.

Etta stood in front of him in her stockings and bloomers, her perky breasts out on display. She covered herself, uncomfortable with his stare, not that he had not seen far more when he and Nanny Mae had shaved her.

Papa took her hands, guiding them down to her sides. "I never want you to feel that you have to hide anything from me, Etta."

His hands grazed her sides and then her hips, gently guiding her bloomers down to her feet.

Etta slipped out of her shoes and then he skimmed down her stockings until she stood in front of him, naked.

Papa turned around, reaching for the examination garment. "Put your hands in here," he said, guiding the gown on. In the back, it remained wide open, giving her an awful breeze on her red bottom. "I see you have had a bit of discipline today."

Embarrassed, Etta averted his stare, her focus on the floor.

Doctor Colt knocked on the door before reentering the examination room. "Climb back up on to the table, child."

She wanted to remind the doctor that she was not a child, but with heavy resignation, she did as she was told. Sitting down was not the hard part. In fact, the beginning of the examination seemed quite easy as the doctor guided his stethoscope beneath the itchy material grazing her skin as he pressed it tightly to her chest.

"Just breathe normally," the doctor said.

She tried to breathe as she usually would, but her heart raced beyond recognition.

Doctor Colt moved the stethoscope from her chest to her back. "Take a deep breath."

Etta did as she was told, breathing in deeply.

"Now let it out."

She followed his instruction again.

"Good." He nodded. "Your heart sounds good. I want to check your temperature. I need you to roll onto your stomach for me, Etta."

Etta locked eyes with her papa.

"Your papa is going to be right here," Doctor Colt reassured her. "Would you like it if he helped with the examination? Would that make it easier?"

Nothing would make it easier, but at least he would not just be watching. "All right," Etta said. She trusted Papa not to hurt her.

Papa Philip helped guide her onto her stomach and then ran his hand gently over her bottom. He separated her cheeks before plunging the thermometer into her rear.

She shifted and struggled against the invasion, pushing it out as quickly as it went in.

"Etta." Papa's voice held a warning note and he swatted her bottom hard. "Stop that!"

The sting of his swat was far more painful than any of Nanny Mae's combined. Papa placed the thermometer at her puckered entrance once more and pushed it back in, holding it in place this time. For something so slim, its presence was quite obvious.

Etta whimpered, trying not to fight him, and was relieved when he removed the thermometer and handed it to Doctor Colt. The doctor glanced at the glass tube. "It is slightly elevated but that is to be expected with her being so nervous. We should check it again tomorrow to make sure it is nothing else."

Tomorrow? Etta had hoped this was a one-time occurrence. She did not want to visit the doctor again, ever. She moved to sit up, but the doctor gently held her shoulder.

"Not yet," he said.

She relaxed onto the table, unsure what was to come next. She tried not to focus on the fact that her bare bum was on full display to the two men.

She looked over her shoulder and saw the doctor moisten his finger with some ointment before gliding it into her bottom, pushing past her pink pucker as he slid his single digit inside. She let out a small squeal at the invasion. Never before—until today—had she had anything, much less a finger, in her back entrance!

"You should begin training this evening, but you will need to go slow. She is quite tight."

Training? What could he possibly be talking about? Dr. Colt pumped his finger in and out a few times and made small circular motions inside, painfully stretching her tiny hole.

"Oh, sir! Please make him stop!"

Papa patted her bottom lightly. "Be a good girl, Etta. Your examination will end soon." His hand spread her cheeks further as it seemed to give him a better view. "Doctor, is it possible for her to take two of your fingers? Please try."

Etta squealed when the doctor complied with Papa's request and attempted to add another. The stretching was too much, and she cried out even louder than before.

"Please, sir! Please. I cannot!"

The doctor paused, but Etta could see from the corner of her eye that Papa had nodded for him to continue—which he did. The second finger was added to the first, and Etta thought she could not endure another moment.

"It is too much! Please remove your fingers," she pleaded as she wiggled her bottom, trying to break free from the intrusion. "It will tear me in half!"

"Shh..." Papa soothed. "Your body will adapt. We have to get your bottom hole ready."

"Ready?" She tried to move off the table, but Papa held her down firmly as Doctor Colt left his two fingers implanted deep within her back channel.

"That is it, child," the doctor praised. "Your bottom is opening for me nicely. If you look closely, Mr. Hartley, you will see how her tiny hole is allowing my fingers to enter, rather than just me pushing them in." His fingers went in deeper, and Etta moaned. "Mr. Hartley, if you would be so kind to reach down and feel her cunny. See if any signs of arousal have occurred, would you?"

Papa did as was asked, and lowered his hand and placed a fingertip to her pussy, which Etta already knew was wet. Her body was clearly betraying her, and she could do nothing more but groan in humiliation as Philip swiped his finger along her folds, collecting her juices.

He removed his hand, brought it to his nose and inhaled. "Yes, Doctor Colt, I believe she is quite aroused."

Heat washed over Etta to the point where she almost felt faint. Doctor Colt began to move his two fingers in and out of her bottom, and Etta couldn't help but moan with a mix of pleasure and pain.

Etta felt restless and was confused that she felt disappointment rather than relief when the doctor removed his fingers and washed his hands. Could the worst of it be over? Maybe the exam was done?

"Roll over, Etta." She awkwardly rolled onto her back, feeling two sets of eyes staring at her as she did so.

Papa stepped closer, taking her hand, showing her that he was not going anywhere.

The doctor gently guided her gown down, getting an eyeful of her breasts as his fingers moved over the mounds and gently pinched a nipple, watching it harden under his touch. "She has a good reaction. Very healthy," the doctor said. "Would you like to try?"

Without hesitation, Papa's hands caressed her breasts, sending a tingle of warmth down between her thighs. Her breathing deepened, each breath slower as she grew more aroused from his touch. His fingers moved down to her stomach, grazing over soft skin before the gown was slipped back over her shoulders.

"I need you to scoot to the bottom of the table," Doctor Colt said.

Etta inched forward, her rear feeling as though she'd fall off at any moment. She kept her legs clamped shut.

"I would like to examine her," Papa said.

"I think it is a good idea for Papa to help. Perhaps you could get her to relax," the doctor said. "It will make it far less painful."

"Look at me," Papa said, his voice stern, his eyes on Etta the entire time. "What do you call me?"

"Papa," she said, knowing the name he preferred to be called.

"Tell me what you want, child."

She wanted to be done with the exam and the room, but another part of her throbbed to be touched. He had grazed her quim and caressed her breasts, paying attention to her like the adult she was, and she craved more from him.

"I want to please you, Papa."

It was exactly what he needed to hear.

"Good," he said. His eyes crinkled with warmth and a smile met his lips. "I need you to relax and do as I say. All right?"

Etta nodded vigorously. Anything to make the exam end.

"Spread your legs wide, Etta." He guided her thighs apart, getting a nice look at her quim, which was now bare, soft, and silky.

She closed her eyes, feeling his touch as he drew a finger between her folds, separating them.

"She is already very wet," the doctor said.

Etta knew that glistening juices spilled from her cunny as her papa barely touched her. Did he know that he was doing this to her?

"Touch her clit. We want to see if you get the desired reaction," Doctor Colt said.

Papa drew his thumb up to her bead, gently circling the hood as it swelled, showing itself to him. "How does that feel?" he asked.

"Really good," she breathed, knowing she needed to be honest. The room felt as though the heat had risen significantly as he pulled his finger from her clit and then stroked her labia, guiding his digits to her entrance.

"Tell me if it hurts," Papa said, sliding a single finger inside her pussy.

She shifted slightly, not from being uncomfortable, but from the desire to feel more, she needed more inside her. No one had ever touched her the way he was doing right now.

"It does not, Papa." She knew he liked to be called that, and she was trying to please him as he did the same for her.

"Good, child. I want you to relax," he said, and guided his finger out, coated in juices before he dipped two fingers inside her virginal cunny. "How is that?"

She squirmed from the fullness. "Nice," she moaned, her eyes staring deep into his. Did he know what he was doing to her? He made her feel as though her world were on fire. He stroked her insides, thrust his fingers in and out as his thumb grazed her clit.

Etta shuddered on the table, wetness seeping between her thighs as her insides clenched down, grasping onto his digits. Her toes curled and heart slammed against her chest as he brought her over the edge toward oblivion.

Gradually his movements slowed before pulling his fingers from her quim. "She is still intact," he said.

Etta closed her eyes, not caring what they were talking about. Her cheeks were red, the room still hot, and her body was covered in a soft pink flush.

"I suggest you get her dressed and put her to bed. She could do with a nap after the day she has had," the doctor said.

Etta did not take naps, but she also did not see the point in arguing. The doctor left the room while Papa helped her put her bloomers on first, his fingers sliding up her legs until he reached her hips. He took a deep breath, backing up as he reached for her dress.

"Lift your arms," he said, guiding the gown back down her body, trapping her breasts and squishing them tight with the material. "We shall leave your shoes and stockings off. Nanny Mae can help you back into those after your nap."

Taking her hand, he led her out of the examining room and down the hall for the nursery.

"Did I pass?" Etta asked.

"What's that, child?"

"Did I pass the exam?" she asked again.

Papa laughed softly, kissing the side of her head. "Indeed, my little Etta, indeed."

He walked her into her room and helped her to the bed. The curtains were shut and the bed turned down, ready for her to climb right in. Etta had not been afforded the luxury of napping since she was a child. With reserve, she climbed between the covers and let her papa cover her up.

"Close your eyes," he said, rubbing her back in a soft soothing motion.

The gesture felt warm and familiar, odd, considering no one had tended to her in years. She had so many questions still, and yet his touch and the exhausting day she had had lulled her toward sleep.

Papa bent down, kissing the top of her head. "Night, child." He quietly slipped from the nursery, closing the door behind him.

TEN

PHILIP'S COCK twitched in his trousers. He had sworn he would wait to touch her until she submitted entirely to him. The same rules he applied to the other papas of the school, he was applying to himself. Except he had broken his rule in helping with the doctor's examination and helping Nanny Mae shave Etta's cunny.

He had not been able to stop himself from doing either, and when Doctor Colt had offered him the chance and opportunity to help, he found himself unable to say no. He did not want to, and by the looks of it, Etta had been glad of it as well. It had eased her mind, or so he thought, helping her relax for the internal exam.

He shifted as he walked down the hall, trying to make himself more comfortable. It did not seem possible. He wanted to take her into his bed and find them both with sated passion, but it would have to wait. She needed to be ready in every way possible, both physically and mentally. He had never seen anyone take to it that quickly, and though she had impressed him with her eagerness to please him by calling him Papa, he also did not want to push things too quickly and scare her away. He needed to tread carefully.

Wandering down the hall, he went to find Nanny Mae. Poking his head into each nursery, he spotted her with another little one.

She sat with Gracie, reading her a story while she sucked on a bottle. Gracie's blonde hair reminded him at first glance of Etta, but he knew it was not her. Gracie was smaller in size and though they were about the same age, she looked much younger.

Nanny Mae helped the child to her feet and tucked her into bed, letting her finish the last drops of the secret formula before pulling it from her lips. "Sweet dreams," she said to Gracie as she quietly closed the bedroom door, joining Philip in the hall. "What can I do for you, Headmaster Philip?"

"How was Etta after she and Leda played together?" Philip asked.

Nanny Mae sighed. "Little Etta was upset, but she would not tell me specifically what happened."

Nanny Vivian tore around the corner of the room, her cheeks flushed. She was visibly out of breath.

Philip's stomach flopped. "What is wrong?" he asked Nanny Vivian.

The young woman looked as though at any moment she might cry. "I lost Leda. I turned my back when I was making the bed for her nap, and she stole out of the room. I cannot find her anywhere!"

The headmaster exhaled a heavy sigh. He should have known that Vivian would not be ready for the responsibilities of being a nanny. She needed to be firm yet gentle when necessary. "We will find her. She could not have gone far." There were more than a dozen rooms, and each held a closet to be searched. He needed to keep Papa Francis from discovering Leda had vanished. Not only would it look bad for the chateau, it would prove that Philip did not have the girls under his control.

Leda needed a good lesson in discipline as soon as they found her, and he would be the perfect one to teach her how to behave as a young girl should.

"We will split up. As soon as you find her, bring Leda to my office."

Philip headed down the hall to make sure the door between the littles and his finishing school was, in fact, still locked. His fingers felt over the jamb, finding it left slightly ajar. "Christ," he cursed under his breath. Perhaps it was just a mere coincidence that the door had been left open and unattended.

He walked from the littles' hall to the highly esteemed finishing school that he was known for being the headmaster of. The doors were shut and he walked past each room, glancing through the clear panes to observe the young women behind their desks.

Though he did not see Leda, he heard a scurrying of footsteps across the marble floor. "Leda," he said, calling to her. "Come to me now and your punishment will not be nearly as harsh as it will if I have to find you myself." He was giving her a chance to receive only the paddle, not the cane as well.

Leda ran past Philip, her fists pounding on the doors of the classrooms as she screamed at the top of her lungs. "He keeps us prisoner as littles for their enjoyment!" She darted from one door to the next, blatantly out of control, until she turned the handle and stepped into one of the classrooms, where the girls were carrying trays of tea and biscuits to a dining table situated in the center of the room.

"We are not for your amusement!" Leda's voice echoed in the small space of the classroom.

"That is enough!" his voice boomed, growing irritated with her display for attention.

She skirted away from Philip, avoiding the girls with trays of food and drinks, but failed to see the teacher coming up behind her. The woman gripped the ruler in her hand and lifted Leda's skirt, smacking her bottom in front of the other pupils.

Leda's eyes widened and she twisted away, trying to break free as Philip stalked into the room and lifted Leda, carrying her over his shoulder.

"Put me down this instant!" She kicked and her arms flailed, trying to beat him as he walked toward the door.

"Ladies!" The teacher clapped her hands, gathering the young girls' attention. "I apologize for the interruption, but it is back to work. Unless you would like to be the next girl with a ruler to her backside?"

Philip forcefully carried Leda through the halls of the finishing school, back toward the door separating the two facets of the chateau. The moment he stepped into the littles' hall, he dropped her hard onto the floor.

She winced, groaning, undoubtedly in pain. That would be nothing compared to the lashing she would get to her bottom.

"Get up, now!" His words echoed through the long hall. He did not dare try and quiet himself.

Nursery doors opened, including Etta's as she stuck her head out, her eyes heavy and filled with sleep. She must have been curious as to what all the fuss was about.

"Go back to bed, girls," Philip said. He leaned down and pulled Leda to her feet, grabbing her by the arm as he swatted her bottom the entire walk back to his office.

Both Nanny Mae and Nanny Vivian breathed a heavy sigh, most likely relieved to see the young woman returned.

Philip shoved Leda into his office and slammed the door shut behind him. He wanted it known how angry he was at her for disobeying the rules. She had been at Ashby long enough to know that sneaking out was prohibited.

"I do not want to be here anymore," Leda said, circling the chair, trying to keep away from the headmaster.

"That is not your choice. You are betrothed to Francis, and he has paid handsomely for your attendance at this institution."

"This place is unbelievable!" Leda shouted at Philip. "Requiring women to dress up as girls. It is insidious." She snarled at her headmaster, showing no signs of remorse for her behavior.

"It is submission, child. You have proven time and time again that you fit right in as a child at Ashby. Perhaps you could learn from the other pupils, like little Gracie, who recognizes authority and submits to her papa. She will be leaving with him next summer, once she completes her committed time with us."

"You cannot make me stay here." Leda headed for the window. From the second story, the windows may have opened, but there were no trees to grasp, no easy way down. Philip had considered every angle when he'd designed the chateau. The first floor housed the cooks, maids, and nannies' sleeping quarters.

"Your guardian signed you over to our care, little Leda."

"Stop calling me that! I am not little!" she shouted at him.

"Perhaps I should bring in your papa. Explain to Francis about your recent behavior and outburst. We could let him determine your fate at Ashby."

Leda shifted on her feet.

"Or you could bare your behind and bend over with your bottom in the air, and accept your punishment like a good little."

Philip was not letting her leave without some level of discipline. Her insubordination needed to be quashed. Whether he provided it, or Francis, she would learn her lesson for causing such an atrocious scene throughout the chateau.

Without a word, Leda bared her little bottom and bent over, touching her ankles. Her dress fell forward, giving Philip a nice glimpse of her crimson backside. It seemed he was not the first one to discipline her this afternoon.

He hated having to resort to the cane, but when girls such as Leda found it impossible to listen, he felt there was no other option. Opening his desk drawer, he removed the long thin stick. With a flick of his wrist, he swatted Leda's bottom, leaving a welt instantly on her bruised rear.

She winced and jumped at the impact. What would teach the girl to behave? Did she need more positive attention from her Papa Francis? Perhaps Philip needed to sit down with the two of them and conduct a meeting to determine what the right course of action would be.

His thoughts returned to Leda's sore backside as he caned her rear again, lower, over her bottom cheeks, near the tops of her legs.

She yelped as the cane landed on her swollen buttocks.

"How many more?" she asked, her voice trembling.

"Until I decide we are done and you thank me for your punishment."

"Thank you?" Leda let go of her ankles and moved to stand up and turn around, when the cane smacked across the tops of her buttocks and she swiftly dropped back to position. "I am sorry."

Philip did not believe her words. He landed another blow to her arse, this one square in the middle of her cheeks. The welt formed as quickly as the cane made contact. "Do not clench," he said, trying to help. "You know it makes the sting last longer."

Whining, she hung her head and started crying.

He hated listening to the tears of the naughty girls, especially when he was not sure which ones were real, and which were an excuse to evade the remainder of their punishment. He would not let her trick him into getting any less swats than she deserved. A firm hand was needed to be a headmaster, and although he didn't always take joy in issuing discipline, it was part of his job, and one that he did not take lightly.

"I am sorry!" she wailed, tears dripping down her face, along with snot.

It was anything but pleasant. Philip gave her three more blows to her bottom before he guided her back up to stand.

She reached down for her bloomers, pulling them back up. "I am sorry I was a naughty girl." Leda wiped the tears away.

"And?" He waited for her to finish, tapping the cane against his palm.

"Thank you for my punishment."

"You're welcome, child." He pointed up to a high-backed, wooden chair facing a corner. "Go sit in the corner on that chair, and think about what you did while I find your papa."

Her eyes widened in fear. Was it sitting on her sore bottom that concerned her, or seeing Francis? Which was worse?

He slipped from the office, locking her inside as he headed down the hall to find her papa.

ELEVEN

ETTA FOUND herself unable to fall back to sleep. After witnessing the display in the hall between Papa and Leda, her stomach was a flurry of butterflies.

Did Papa discipline all the littles? She hated to feel the surge of jealousy that coursed through her tummy. She wanted him all to herself.

Slipping out of the nursery, she wandered down the hall and paused as she watched Philip storm out of his office, heading the opposite direction.

She breathed a sigh of relief. Curious as to what was going on, she crept toward his office until she could see through the frosted glass that someone was inside the room. It had to be Leda. Etta tried the door but it was locked.

"Leda?" Etta hissed, giving a faint knock.

"Who is there?" Leda asked.

"It's me, Etta." She knew she would get into trouble if they were caught, but she wanted to hear what had happened from Leda. Would her papa tell her the truth?

"Go away," Leda said, making no attempt to get up from her seat in the corner.

Etta sat down, her back to the door. "I do not know what you did, but my papa is really mad at you."

Leda did not answer her.

"I want you to stop being bad," Etta said. "My papa shouldn't be disciplining you. He should be paying attention to me."

Leda laughed from the other side of the door. "You are jealous?"

Yes. Etta did feel the strings of jealousy tugging at her insides, making her displeased.

From down the hall, footsteps were fast approaching. She needed to head back to her room, or she could end up with her own bruised bottom.

"It is a grave disappointment," Philip said as he came nearer.

"Stop seeking attention!" Etta hissed at Leda, before rushing back into her room, shutting the door, and throwing herself under the covers in case anyone noticed. She pretended to be asleep. Etta shut her eyes and wished away all the bad things that happened in the world. Right now, her one main thought was of Leda. Why did she have to try and ruin Etta's happiness?

The nursery door squeaked open.

"Etta?" Nanny Mae's soft voice could be heard as she entered the room.

"I am asleep," Etta mumbled, wanting to fall back to sleep. If it weren't for her papa waking her and Leda causing trouble, she probably would have still been asleep. She wanted to go back to dreamland, where everything was peaceful and she did not worry about disappointing anyone.

"I know for a fact that is not true. I saw you in the hall just a few minutes ago."

Etta had not seen Nanny Mae. Her eyes flashed open and she rolled over to face her nanny. "Am I in trouble?"

"Well, that depends. What were you doing out in the hall on your own?" she asked.

Lying seemed a bad idea, but could the truth save her? "Papa woke me when he was yelling at Leda." Perhaps that had been when Nanny Mae had seen her with the door open. Etta hoped she had not been caught sneaking down the hall to her papa's office.

"I know, dear. Sometimes good littles do very naughty things. It is why they are here at Ashby, to help them remember that their papa is in charge, and they are to do as he says, always."

Etta sat up in bed, pushing the covers off. Her room felt hot, or maybe it was the concern creeping up on her about being caught that had her flushed.

"I need you to climb off the bed and pull your bloomers down."

"What? Why?" Etta asked.

"Your papa asked me to get you started on your training. No more questions." Nanny Mae waited for Etta to do as she was told.

Etta climbed off the bed and slowly lowered her bloomers to the floor.

"Good girl. Now lean forward toward the bed, with your bottom out in the air." Nanny Mae helped guide Etta into position. "Spread your legs further apart."

"Nanny Mae?" Etta's voice caught in her throat, nervous after what she had been through with the doctor earlier. There were some things she had not liked about the exam and others she had found oddly satisfying. What did her nanny plan to do with her?

The nanny grabbed a small black leather box and pulled from it a glass object, along with a jar of lubricant. "This will make you a little more comfortable, child." Nanny Mae poured a generous amount of wetness onto her fingers before she spread Etta's cheeks, sticking her finger into her pink pucker, just as the doctor had. "You need to relax." Nanny Mae lightly spanked Etta's pussy with her other hand.

"What is that glass item?" Etta asked, enjoying the slight sting to her sex caused by the light pussy swats.

Wetness seeped between her thighs, and her lips opened as she began to breathe more heavily, as her quim tingled. Her breasts felt fuller and weightier as Nanny Mae swiped her fingers over her folds, surely able to feel the heat radiating from her body.

"It is a plug to stretch your arsehole for your papa," Mae said.

"What?" Etta squeaked as she tried to hold back the moans of pleasure the spanking to her cunny caused.

Just as she felt she may explode, the spanking stopped, and Nanny Mae coated the entire plug with the ointment before separating Etta's round rosy cheeks again. "Just relax. Imagine it is your papa claiming you, child," the woman said.

Claiming her? Surely her papa would never put his... his member inside her *there*!

Slowly, Nanny Mae inched the plug into her bottom.

Etta panted, groaning as it stretched her tiny hole. Her quim pulsed from the insertion of the plug into her backside. She wanted Papa to cuddle her and feel his fingers enter her wetness again. "When will I see Papa again?" she asked.

As the plug was pushed as far as it would go, Etta felt a sharp pain, and then a sense of relief once it had been seated snugly inside. Nanny Mae patted her bottom. "You can stand up now."

Etta repositioned herself on the floor, dragging her legs closer together in slow methodical movements. She could still feel the plug in her behind, making her cunny ache even more. Her hips rocked and her fingers snaked down toward her clit, wanting to feel more than just a plug in her bottom. She craved a second release for that day.

Nanny Mae did not appear pleased to see what her charge was doing. She smacked her hands away and pushed her back onto the mattress, pinning her down, hovering above her.

Etta stared up at her nanny, her eyes as dark as night, the pupils looking huge. "You will not touch yourself again, is that clear?"

Nanny Mae smacked Etta's quim.

Etta moaned, finding it both satisfying and further arousing.

Her nanny's eyes widened in surprise. "Did you just moan?"

Etta nodded, she did not see the point in lying. Nanny Mae could see how excited her body was. Her breasts strained against the sailor outfit and her quim throbbed to be touched. Her sweet womanly odor poured from between her thighs, filling the room with the smell of sex.

Nanny Mae slipped her fingers between Etta's legs. She leaned down until her lips were covering Etta's ear. "If you tell anyone, especially your papa about this, you will never be able to sit on your bottom again."

Etta silently swore her promise. She gave a nod, all she could do to satisfy herself.

Nanny Mae stroked Etta's sex, her fingers rubbing hard and with long strokes, pinching and pulling at her labia as her thumb circled her clit.

Etta's lips parted and she threw her head back, her eyes slamming shut as the second orgasm began to rip through her body. She lifted her hips, grinding against Nanny Mae's hands, desiring and craving more, but that was all that could be offered.

"Please," Etta begged, needing the aching throb to dull or fearing she might otherwise find herself with a knife-like pain through the heart. She leaned up, finding Nanny Mae's mouth, and placing her own over the woman's soft perfect cherry lips. The woman tasted exactly the way she smelled, of vanilla and spice. Etta's tongue pushed past Nanny Mae's lips as she shuddered in her nanny's arms.

Collapsing against the mattress, Etta's heart felt as though it might explode.

Nanny Mae climbed off the young woman's body, smoothed down her dress, and picked up Etta's bloomers from the floor. "Put these back on, along with your stockings and shoes. It is time to visit the playroom with the other littles."

Etta did not want to go anywhere except back to bed. It took every ounce of strength to finish dressing.

Nanny Mae waited by the door, avoiding Etta's stare.

Once Etta was dressed, Nanny Mae took her by the hand and led her down the hall. Would her papa know what they had done? She did not want to get her nanny fired from Ashby. Etta found that she liked it—and Nanny Mae—very much.

She scampered into the playroom, grateful to be among other littles and away from the nannies and papas for a while.

TWELVE

IT TOOK Philip hours to settle down after Leda had put his heart into a state of fury. Reddening her bottom had been beneficial to both of them, but it had not eradicated the problem entirely. He would have Nanny Vivian keep a closer eye on Leda, and if she could not handle it, Vivian would be out of a job.

He needed to calm down, and the best place to do that was to keep an eye on the nursery, watching his new little one playing amongst the others. From behind the glass, he studied her features. Etta's cheeks were flushed, far rosier than he had ever seen them before.

Frowning, he headed in through the door and knelt down to her level as she sat on the floor. "Are you feeling all right, Etta?" The back of his hand shot out, feeling over her forehead. She felt warm to the touch, which explained her complexion. Undoubtedly, she was running a fever. During her exam earlier, her temperature had been slightly elevated, and he intended to check it again tomorrow. He kissed the top of her head before retreating to get a thermometer. Perhaps it was time to take her temperature again and make sure it was not as high as he thought.

Philip returned after a few minutes, the glass tube in his hand. "Etta, I am going to need to take your temperature."

"Here?" she squeaked with wide eyes as she glanced at the other littles.

Yes, he knew it would probably embarrass her, but she needed to learn to submit to him, and feeling humility would help that process. What better way than to have her cheeks spread and her temperature taken for all to see?

Philip took a seat on one of the wooden chairs that the nannies often used while the children were playing. "Come here," he said. His voice was stern and his tone showed no hint of humor as her feet remained planted firmly on the playroom floor. "If I have to get up, your bottom will not only see a thermometer."

Etta swallowed nervously and inched closer, as slow as treacle. When she was within reach, he held out his arm, grabbed her wrist, and pulled her unceremoniously toward him. "Bend over," he said, offering his legs as support for her stomach.

With slow abandon, she lay face down across his legs, her head pointing toward the floor. The warmth only seemed to further radiate from her body as he pushed her bloomers down to her knees. Surprised to find a plug already in her bottom, he did his best to hide the smile on his face and the swell growing in his trousers.

"I see you have begun training with Nanny Mae." He spread her cheeks and slowly guided the plug out of her. That could not be the cause of her fever? No. Philip felt confident that something else was going on. Perhaps she had a touch of something she had picked up at her uncle's place. It had been covered in a sheen of dust and the weather had been damp.

Philip shook the thermometer before spreading Etta's bottom cheeks, sliding the glass tube in past her pink pucker.

Every ounce of her skin that he grazed felt warm. Her bottom was covered in a pink blush, though he knew that had more to do with her punishments from earlier.

She squirmed and moaned. Philip smacked her sharply. "Hold still, child." He was not in the mood to deal with a second little who would defy him that afternoon. It had been an exhausting day and he wanted it over. Besides, the thermometer should have been easier for her to take after having worn the plug. How long had she been training with it? Had Nanny Mae just put it in?

"I do not want to!" Etta whined like a child, trying to break free.

Why was she acting this way? She had been more compliant in the doctor's office. He landed a second smack and then a third to her bottom, forcing her to clench as she pushed at the thermometer. Philip pushed it right back in, not letting her be done yet.

"You will be here longer the more you resist," he said.

Etta stopped thrashing, her face buried down toward the floor.

He waited a solid three minutes from the time she stopped fussing until he removed the glass tube, examining the markings. Her temperature was still elevated, but not as high as he expected it to be. Even so, he pulled up her bloomers and helped Etta to her feet. He would introduce a bigger plug to fill her bottom before bed. "Come with me," he said, his tone short and abrupt.

He took Etta by the hand, her face no less red than when he had laid eyes on her in the playroom. "I am taking you to the nursery," he said. Fluids and a cool bath would do her a world of good.

"I am not tired, Papa."

He knew she had recently awoken from her nap, and perhaps that explained a bit of the rise in temperature, but he had caught a waft of her cunny as he had her bent over his knee. It was as if she were in heat, her sex hot and swollen, begging to be touched. Although he wanted to graze her quim, listen to her squirm and moan, she was not ready for it. Pleasure was a reward, and she needed to be well and healthy before he took her down a path they could not return from.

"Nanny Mae!" He gestured her nanny over, snapping his fingers into the air to get her attention.

The red-haired, fair-skinned woman excused herself from the ladies and walked up to Headmaster Philip.

"Etta is running a slight fever. It started before her nap, but I was expecting it to have disappeared. I would like you to give her a cold bath and then a bottle. Put her down to bed, and go up a size in your training. I shall come to check on her later."

"Do not go," Etta said, her voice soft and fragile.

Philip wanted to stay, and staring at her beautiful blue eyes only tugged on his heart, making the choice that much harder. "You need your rest."

"I do not feel ill. Just hot."

"I know. You are running a fever." Philip nodded in understanding. He recognized that she undoubtedly did feel hot. "Does your head hurt?" Usually a headache accompanied a fever.

"No, Papa."

He kissed her forehead. She seemed cooler than earlier. "Come." He took her hand and led her into the washroom, with Nanny Mae trailing behind. The porcelain claw tub sat in the center of the room.

"Undress," he commanded Etta.

She stood there, not moving.

"Listen to your papa," Nanny Mae said, chastising the girl. She swatted her bottom for not following directions.

"Get some cool water. I want to bring down Etta's temperature and then give her a bottle before bed," Philip said.

"What about dinner?" Etta asked.

Nanny Mae retrieved the water bucket and headed out of the room to fill it with cool tepid water. She slowly began to fill the bathtub.

"You will get enough of the nutrients you need from a bottle. I want you healthy for tomorrow."

"What is happening tomorrow?" Etta asked, continuing with the questions.

He waited for her to undress. When she did not move fast enough, he reached for her hips, pulling her toward him. "Arms up."

Etta lifted her arms above her head, and Philip tugged the material up over her head, letting it fall to the floor. She reached to cover her breasts and he spanked her bottom. "Do not hide yourself from me. Put your hands down."

Slowly, she lowered her hands along with her gaze as her perky breasts and peaked nipples revealed themselves to him.

Philip tried to hide the discomfort in his trousers as his cock hardened at the sight of her beautiful body. His fingers grazed her hips, inching the bloomers down past her slick folds and to her feet for her to climb out from. Her quim appeared a luscious pink and red, her clit visibly sticking out and swollen. He'd never seen a little this aroused—at least, not one who had not been with her papa.

"Have you been touching yourself, child?" Philip's voice was stern, his eyes narrowed as he glared at her disapprovingly.

Etta shook her head.

"Do not lie to me!"

"I swear I have not."

What had aroused Etta to make her pearl swell so fully and her quim glisten with wetness?

Philip caught Nanny Mae's fearful gaze as the woman stared at Etta. Had something transpired between the two of them? He had known his nannies to discipline the girls. Perhaps the tough display had aroused his little Etta.

Nanny Mae cleared her throat. "May I have a word with you outside?"

Philip glanced from a naked Etta to the nanny. "Stay here, Etta. We shall be right back." He stalked out of the room with Nanny Mae and shut the door to the nursery. "Would you like to tell me what is going on?"

"Perhaps if we went into your office," Nanny Mae said, stammering.

He cleared his throat and shuffled down the hall, opening the door to his private office. "Come in. Sit down." He assumed it would not take just a minute if she wanted only him to hear what had to be said.

"I would rather stand." She rested her hands on the back of the chair.

"That was not a question." Philip was always in charge. Not just to the littles, but he also held a wealth of power over the nannies. "Sit."

Nanny Mae nodded her understanding and walked around to sit in the upholstered chair. "I believe I know why your little is showing signs of arousal," she said.

"Do you?" His expression grew grim. "If she is touching herself, you know that the responsibility lies with you to stop her."

"I know, and I made a mistake," Mae said.

"What kind of mistake?" Philip asked. He came to stand in front of Nanny Mae, perching on the edge of the wooden desk. "Elaborate." He did not ask her kindly, as it had been her duty to keep Etta in line.

"I may have gone to restrain her after she touched her quim, but then, I do not know how to explain what happened..." Her words trailed off and her cheeks burned as she stared down at her hands in her lap. "I may have been the cause of that source of arousal."

"You?" Philip pushed himself further from the desk. "I trusted you with my little Etta."

"I know." Nanny Mae nodded. "And I assure you it was consensual."

"That is beside the point. As a little at this school, she has given up the right to make decisions for herself. That is why she is here, to learn to regress as a child would. Abusing her does not fit into our curriculum!"

Nanny Mae's eyes shot up to meet his and she sat up straighter. "I did *not* abuse Etta." Her words were terse and she gritted her teeth, seething.

"Do you love her?" Philip was not sure he even wanted to hear the answer. Etta was his little one and no one else's.

"As a little, but nothing more," Nanny Mae said, shaking her head. "I do not know what came over me."

Philip had a pretty good idea what had come over her. She had grown heated and filled with lust. Staring at a woman's breasts and quim, spanking her —all had finally got to her in the same way it got to him. Not that he could tell her that. He could not be all right with what had happened. There had to be consequences, but firing her did not feel appropriate. "You will work in the eastern wing from now on. I do not want you to see Etta again, is that clear?"

"Thank you, Headmaster Philip."

She had to know he had saved her job, and a small part of him loved Mae in a way that showed affection and warmth, like a child loved a precious doll. She had been the security that he had needed to ensure him time to grow, accept his role as headmaster, and now as papa. He needed a nanny for Etta, but it would not be Nanny Mae. Her time with the littles was over.

THIRTEEN

ETTA STOOD stark naked in the lonely bathroom. Papa and Nanny Mae had left her alone, but for what reason? Were they going to discuss what had happened between her and Nanny Mae after her nap?

The door creaked open, and Etta stared at Papa as he stalked into the room, looking displeased.

"Where is Nanny Mae?" she asked.

"Gone." He gave her no hint of anything further.

Etta's brow furrowed and the first hint of tears surfaced in her eyes. She had not been fond of Nanny Mae at first glance, but the woman had worn her down, and she respected her. "Where did she go?"

"That is not for you to worry about," Papa said. "You will have a new nanny looking after you by tomorrow. In the meantime, I am going to take care of you."

Her heart skipped a beat. She would much rather have Papa look after her. "Do I have to have a new nanny?" She'd even be pleased to have Nanny Mae back. She was not so bad, and Etta did not have the slightest clue who else Papa would hire. Would it be someone worse, with harsher discipline and a stricter hand to her bottom?

"Yes, child. I cannot watch over you and the entire chateau without a little help." He kissed the top of her head. "Your fever seems to have broken. Let's get you into your nightgown and climb into bed."

"I am not tired," Etta said, whining. It was nearing dinner time and her stomach grumbled for food. She didn't dare remind him that the bottle had been forgotten.

"Do not disappoint me," Papa said, his tone stern and sharp. He walked into the nursery and found a light pink nightgown for her to wear to bed. "Arms up."

Etta did not fight him. Perhaps if she did as she was told, he'd see that she did not need another nanny, that she could be trusted to be on her own. She was a grown adult, even if he seemed to forget that about her. Lifting her arms into the air, she let him guide the soft pink nightgown over her head and arms.

"Come." Papa guided Etta to the bed and pulled back the covers. "Lie on your tummy," he said, instructing her on what to do.

She climbed atop the mattress, burying her fingers under the pillow as she laid her head down, her bottom facing the ceiling.

"Seeing as you are not ill as we first thought, I think it is best to leave the cold bath away."

"What is wrong with me?" Etta did not understand why she felt so warm. Her quim burned and the clothes felt too hot and restrictive, even just a simple nightgown.

"You are aroused, Etta. Nanny Mae should not have done what she did, but I hear you were a naughty girl, touching yourself. Is that what started it?"

Etta did not answer.

Papa lifted the hem of her gown, exposing her round bottom as his fingers moved over the plush curves. "Naughty girls get paddled."

Etta snapped her head around to study Papa's stern expression. "Paddled?"

Papa reached for the drawer of the dresser beside the bed and opened it. Etta gasped when she watched him pull out a wooden paddle.

"What happened between you and Nanny Mae deserves a punishment. You are not to touch yourself, and you most certainly are not to allow anyone to touch you unless I say so."

Without hesitation, he laid the paddle on her backside so she could feel the cool wood against her heated bare flesh. Etta had never been paddled, but undoubtedly this experience was not one she would enjoy. But before she could plead for mercy or even come up with an escape plan, the paddle raised and then came crashing down on her arse with a stinging blow.

"Ow! Oh, Papa!" Another searing swat landed on her bottom. "It hurts!"

"Yes, my little love, I'm afraid a proper paddling is indeed going to sting."

He continued to paddle her bottom without pause, and Etta could do nothing more but wail in pain. The thud of each spank almost took her breath away, as her papa delivered a paddling she would not soon forget.

"I am so sorry, Papa. I will never do such things again!"

The paddling continued.

"Yes, little Etta, I will make sure of that."

The paddling continued.

"Ow! Ow! I cannot take anymore. I simply cannot!"

The paddling continued.

"I do not like punishing you so harshly," he said as he landed two more swats on each cheek and then stopped. "But it is my duty, as your papa, to do so when it is deserved. You nearly cost a woman her job, Etta. Her livelihood is not a game."

Etta sniffed and tried to dry her tears. She knew she indeed deserved her paddling. Her behavior had not been that of a lady.

Papa put the paddle down and caressed her bottom gently. "Do you understand why you are at the Ashby Chateau, Etta?"

"I am to find a suitable man to marry." That was why her Uncle Jack had sent her away. He did not seem to know anything about girls or young women, so he had pushed her out of the door as fast as she had come into his home.

"You are to learn to submit, Etta. I want you to recognize the power and give it up entirely to me. I am going to claim you as my wife when the time comes, my little love."

Etta swallowed nervously. "You wish to marry me?" Had he lost his mind? She had suspected as much because of the talk from Nanny Mae, but she had pushed it aside and could have sworn that he would never want someone like her.

"Everything about you is perfect, except your submission. Please me, and I will do everything in my power to make you pleased. Now relax," he said.

From the corner of her eye, she could see Papa pull out a jar of ointment from the same drawer the paddle had been in, which made her tummy do a flip. His hands came to separate her cheeks before he dipped a single digit into her bottom. "Take it in, imagine it is me inside you."

Softly she moaned, her eyes slamming shut as he stirred the strange desire she had never felt before arriving at Ashby. Since then, her body had come alive in ways she never knew possible, and it happened more than once a day.

"That is a good girl. You are still so tight, though," he said, pushing a second digit inside her tight hole.

Etta shifted her hips and he removed his fingers, opening the drawer of the nightstand beside the bed. Taking out an item that Etta already recognized, he added some ointment before sliding a new plug into her bottom. This one felt bigger and stretched her as it eased inside her rear. Whimpering, she wanted the pain to stop.

"Relax," he said. "It will not hurt any more than it already does."

The pain was mixed with pleasure and as she felt her bottom completely full, he rolled her onto her back. "Spread your legs, Etta."

Licking her dry lips, she followed his command. Whatever he said, she would do. She wanted to please him and, more importantly, she did not want a replacement nanny tomorrow.

Wetness coated her quim and Papa bent down to her level, examining her folds as he spread them apart.

It felt strange to have someone staring so intimately at a place that no one had ever examined before today.

"I am going to kiss you," Papa said.

She expected him to climb up her body and cover her lips with his own, but instead his mouth descended onto the heat and fire down below. His breath tickled her bare skin as his fingers separated her folds further, licking her swollen nub.

Etta's bottom tightened on the plug, her cunny pulsating as he licked and sucked her bead of nerves that sent her shuddering on the mattress.

He guided two fingers into her wetness, stroking her as she trembled beneath him.

Her breathing grew in intensity, her heart slammed against the walls of her chest, begging to break free, as if her heart and emotions were imprisoned. She moaned, and her papa did not try and silence her pleas. Wetness coated his fingers and dripped from her pussy as he licked and sucked, drinking all of it in.

Etta's toes curled and her quim clenched around his digits. She wished there was more to fill her, not just the plug in her bottom but his cock in her quim. Would he ever give her what she desired? Was he waiting until they were actually married? He had seen she was still a virgin, her maidenhead being intact during the examination. What was he waiting for?

"I want you," she said, her words thick and filled with longing. Her fingers clung to his shirt, pulling it from his trousers, ready to undress him and pin him beneath her, though she doubted he would ever let her be in control.

Climbing back up her body, he gently guided the gown down past her exposed quim and kissed her cheeks and nose, staring down at her with a smile. She softly moaned when she could smell her own essence on his breath.

"Good."

Etta did not know what that meant. Was he pleased with what had happened? He took a deep breath, pulled the covers up around her, and then lay down on the mattress atop the blankets, his hand draped across her waist.

Her eyes shut and she did not bother to ask about her next meal. She had no desire to drink from a bottle and felt that if she climbed from the bed, her legs would give out. Etta knew she would collapse, feeling wobbly as she needed her rest.

"Goodnight, my little love," he said, whispering the words into her ear. "I shall wake you for dinner."

There was no clock and the sky had darkened, but it was winter. It was much too hard to tell the hour. She drifted off to sleep, needing the rest, whether it was for twenty minutes or two hours. Feeling his strong arms surrounding her, Etta felt safe, comforted, and pleased.

FOURTEEN

HOW COULD Nanny Mae have betrayed him? As Etta fell asleep in his arms, the silence enveloping them only seemed to stir his anger and hatred for what she had done to his little one. Etta was *his,* and though he may not have claimed her yet, no one was supposed to bring her to her knees and make her quiver in ecstasy but him.

Philip hated himself for letting Nanny Mae get that close and not noticing. How many other littles had she taken advantage of? Though she claimed it had been consensual, had it really been, or had Etta felt she had no other choice?

Etta mumbled in her sleep and as he moved to pull away, he changed his mind and stroked the blonde tresses out of her face instead. Beneath the blankets, she was warm, nearly sticky from sweat. Was she having a bad dream? He tried to soothe her, his hands caressing her cheeks and down her back.

"Papa?" she whispered, her eyes slowly opening as she wiped away the few remnants of tears. He had been correct, she had been having a bad dream. Usually the little's nanny took care of such rare occurrences, but it was his job this evening.

"Do you want to tell me about your dream?" he asked, sitting up in bed.

Etta pushed the covers down to her waist, sitting up with him. Sadness crept over her features like a dark rain cloud from above. "It was awful." She stared down at the quilt, her fingers caressing the delicate pattern.

Philip lifted her chin to meet his gaze. "What was awful, Etta?"

"Watching my father die."

He understood the severity of her pain and the fact that the dream was more real than she would have hoped. "I am sorry about your father," he said, his eyes staring longingly into her ocean blue gaze.

"Me too." Her bottom lip trembled and as she tried to avoid his stare, her face found the crook of his neck, her tears soaking through his shirt. She sobbed and unleashed a fury of tears that had been stored in her heart for the loss of her family.

Philip had known this day would come. That sadness and grief would meet her head on. He was not fond of watching girls cry, but he would comfort her, shoulder her pain, and help her move on, hopefully with him. He wanted to make her happy and prayed she desired the same.

His large hands stroked her back over the gown.

She pressed into him, tighter, her fingers clutching his shirt as if it were her life preserver and she were in a rough sea, struggling to survive. Etta gasped, finding it hard to breathe, as if water choked her lungs as the waves lapped above her head, drowning her.

He pulled her into his lap, his arms strong and warm as he tried his best to comfort her. Rocking her softly, he cradled her like a child in his embrace and listened as she hiccupped, her breathing slowly returning to normal. His touch calmed and soothed, his kisses soft and gentle against her neck as he kept her pressed close to him. He wanted to erase her pain, ease her suffering and her loss. He did not know what else to do. Many of the girls who came to the chateau had a history of difficulty and troublesome behavior, but few had lost one parent, and none except for Etta had lost both.

She was his special little. Unlike the other girls who struggled to fit in, Etta's only clash was with her past. It would always be there, a reminder of a life that she had lost. She would need to move on, let go of the pain and accept her place at Ashby. He'd yet to decide what to do with her upon her graduation. It was still quite some time away, but he'd need to develop a plan for Etta that would keep her happy. Part of that meant knowing who she was, what she loved, and what she needed. He needed her submission, it was what Philip craved, but what did she desire? What would keep her loyal only to him?

"Thank you." Her soft voice broke the silence.

He did not release his hold on her yet, keeping her in his arms a moment longer before feeling her struggle.

"What's wrong?"

She glanced at the door to the washroom. "I need to—"

"You need to what?" he asked. She had not finished her sentence, and he was not waiting until tomorrow for her to answer.

"I need to use the potty."

He helped her down from bed and walked with her into the washroom where the chamber pot sat. "Do I need to help you?" Philip was not sure what Nanny Mae did when it came to using the potty. There were some aspects of being a little that he preferred to let the nannies handle. This was one of them.

Etta smiled politely. "I can handle it."

He nodded and stepped out of the washroom, heading for the door. Philip's stomach protested that he had not eaten dinner yet. "Get dressed again, in the clothes you were wearing earlier today. I shall be outside your door in ten minutes." He gave her plenty of time to change while he checked to see if dinner was ready. She would need a nanny, since he had dismissed Nanny Mae from her responsibilities as Etta's caretaker. Nanny Vivian was still new and learning the trade, but perhaps she could step in until he found someone else. Who, though? That was always a difficult question, since he tried to keep his school of littles and their discipline discreet. Perhaps bringing one of the young women from the east wing to the littles' hall would be best. He'd have to choose someone who had instilled discipline in the girls, and yet also knew how to keep her hands to herself when appropriate.

Yes. He knew just the person. Elizabeth had been a governess for a private household before coming to Ashby Chateau. She was the first introduction most girls had to a teacher, every new pupil spent several hours with her, getting acquainted with the rules before being placed in the appropriate class. Her job, though undoubtedly important, would serve her well to keep his littles in line. For Elizabeth, the ruler was practically attached to her hand, another appendage that she found it necessary to keep on her at all times. She scared even him, her stern gaze, rough accent, and thick-bodied proportions made him feel inadequate. She was the nanny that no little would want but all would submit to. At least, that was what Philip hoped.

He headed down the hall, unlocked the door to the east wing, and went to find Elizabeth. Would she be willing to join the littles and keep them in line? Her direction and guidance were a valuable asset that the chateau had, and removing her from the finishing school would be a great loss, but a necessary one.

FIFTEEN

ETTA FINISHED GETTING DRESSED. Even though Philip had told her to dress once more in that ridiculous sailor's outfit, she decided to take a moment to try and find a gown more suitable for dinner. All the dresses were above the knee, revealing far more than she thought appropriate. With the ugly white bloomers destined to poke out from the bottom of every hem, she had no choice but to choose a gown fit for a child.

She pulled the material over her head, the bright pink blinding and definitely not her color, but she wore it anyway. There weren't any gowns in the armoire that she found appealing. Would her papa ever bring her one that she did like? For how long was he expecting to keep her at the chateau? Certainly not as long as Leda, she hoped.

She secured the white stockings up past her knees. At the top a black bow sat on her mid-thigh. She slipped on the black shoes she had worn earlier and walked toward the door. Was she supposed to find Papa, or was he coming back for her? Etta could not remember. She had only been half paying attention to what he had been saying.

Opening the door, she poked her head out into the hall. "Papa?" Etta called, her voice drifting down the corridor.

The familiar click of heels on marble forced Etta back into her room.

"I expect quite an increase in pay for this, Headmaster Philip," a woman's voice barked at her papa.

"Yes. Of course," Philip said.

Etta closed the door and shuffled toward the bed, sitting down on the edge just as the strange woman came into her room.

"Get up!" the woman commanded Etta. She stalked toward her, pulling her by the arm onto her feet. "Let me look at you."

"I am Etta," she said, trying to be polite and introduce herself. Did this woman have no manners?

"I know who you are," the woman said. A slight gap nestled between her two front teeth, causing a slight hiss as she spoke. Etta felt certain she would feel a spray of spit, but it never came. "Is this what your nanny dressed you in?" She glanced Etta up and down, disapprovingly.

"Nanny Mae had her dressed in a sailor's outfit, which I told her to put back on," Papa answered.

Why was he helping this woman? Etta did not like her. Already she smelled of medicine and her tone seemed harsh. If Etta was a little, shouldn't this woman be good with children? It seemed she hated them—and her—already.

"She decided to change without permission?" The woman grabbed Etta by the waist, hoisted her over her lap and pulled down her bloomers, revealing her recently paddled backside.

The woman took charge, spanking Etta's poor bare bottom, reddening it even more than it had been on contact.

Etta's legs kicked and she squirmed, trying to break free from this beast of a woman. Who the blazes was she? She was not anything like Nanny Mae, who had been dainty and quite beautiful. This woman had muscles that could have easily been a man's, thick and robust. Her dark short curly hair sat atop her head like a mop.

"Let me go!" Etta cried, tears running down her face. What had she done to upset this woman? Not even two minutes with her, and she was getting disciplined.

The woman kept spanking Etta, giving no indication that she would let up anytime soon.

"Good little girls listen to their nanny," she barked.

When had she not listened to Nanny Mae? "I do!" Etta shrieked. She thrashed against the woman, only receiving more blows to her rapidly swelling bottom. At this rate, she would never be able to sit down again.

"Do you enjoy disobeying your papa?" the woman asked.

Etta had not thought she had done anything wrong. She'd been good, even when she had not enjoyed having a plug in her bottom or receiving a thorough examination from the doctor. "I *have* been good!" she wailed, her cheeks clenching with each swat as another hard slap was released. "Ow!" she reached behind her to stop the madness, finding her hands getting smacked and pushed together up above her head. Why did her papa not try and defend her? Just because she had decided to try and find something more suitable to wear for dinner?

"Good little girls do not fight me, child." The woman's voice came out as a hiss, sounding angry.

Why was the woman so furious? "I am sorry," Etta said, the tears wetting her face on their descent down her cheeks and to the floor, each droplet coating the marble floor that she'd step upon shortly.

"What are you sorry for?" the woman asked, her hand in the air, waiting to spank Etta again if she gave the wrong answer.

Etta lifted her head, her eyes finding Papa glancing out of the window. Had she disgusted him so much that he did not dare look at her?

"I am sorry, Papa." She did not want to disappoint him. He had taken her into Ashby, looked out for her in the only way he knew how, and kept her safe. It was more than she would have on the streets. Her Uncle Jack may have been paying room and board, but it was Papa who had been taking care of her.

"You are forgiven," Papa said, turning to face Etta. "You will obey my instructions in future, and listen to Nanny Beth from now on. Is that clear?"

Etta nodded. She did not want to listen to this new nanny, let alone have a nanny at all, but it seemed her papa was too busy for her. Etta recognized that he had a job to do, to care for all the girls at the chateau, but she wanted to be the only one he noticed. She wanted his undivided attention. If it were up to her, she would find every way possible to make Nanny Beth's life utterly miserable.

He kissed Etta's cheek before untangling her from Nanny Beth's embrace and helping her to stand.

"Where are you going?" Etta asked as he headed for the door.

"I have some business to attend to." He locked eyes with Nanny Beth. What was going on? What had happened to Nanny Mae? Had she been fired? If Etta had just not been so hot and flushed, no one would have known what had happened between them. Regret filled every ounce of Etta's heart. She had not meant to get Nanny Mae fired.

"Sit with Etta. Make sure she eats her vegetables like a good girl." Papa did not wait for a response as he headed out of the nursery.

"Come, little one. We have not got all day." Nanny Beth's tone was sharp and when Etta did not jump quickly enough, she grabbed Etta by the arm, dragging her toward the door. One hand gripped Etta's arm, the other hand landed a rough blow to her bottom again. "You will listen and do as I say."

Dragging Etta down the hall, Beth's pace was swift as she seemed to glide with ease. Etta could have sworn the woman was a witch. Her feet didn't even seem to touch the ground. Even though she could not see Beth's shoes because the gown she was wearing reached the floor, it appeared as though she floated effortlessly. Already Etta was coming to despise Nanny Beth. She had no desire to give her an honest chance, either.

Standing in the dining hall was a young man in his late twenties or early thirties, in a pinstripe suit and donning a hat. His hair was as black as coal and his eyes as dark as night. "I am here for Henrietta Waters."

Etta shuffled her feet, pulling away from Nanny Beth's grasp. "That is me," Etta said. "I am Henrietta. Who are you?" She may have hated to be called by her given name, but the chance of a reprieve from her new nanny made her jump at the opportunity to be Henrietta once again.

"Do not talk to the little one. You do your business with the headmaster or the other papas." Nanny Beth stalked closer to the strange gentleman. "The littles are to be left alone."

A confused look crossed the man's face. He shook his head, dismissing her questions. "I am here for Henrietta." Reaching into his jacket pocket, he retrieved a document, handing it to Nanny Beth for her examination. "She is to be my wife. I am taking her from this establishment at once. I have already spoken to Headmaster Philip. He assured me that you would hand her over without reservation."

Nanny Beth quietly read through the piece of paper, taking in the information without a word.

"What?" Etta's eyes widened. "This cannot be." She did not even know this man! Had she done something to disappoint Papa so badly that he had married her off to the first available bachelor whose path he crossed? Had that been why he had not stopped Nanny Beth from spanking her? Did he believe she had been a bad little one?

"I see," Nanny Beth said, still examining the paper in her hands.

"You can't make me go with you!" Etta took a step back. She refused to leave with a stranger. Her papa owed her the decency of saying goodbye if he wanted her gone and out of his hair.

"Actually, Henrietta, I can. I have the paperwork that permits us to be married at once."

"No." Etta shook her head, her eyes wide. She didn't believe him. "You are a liar!" There was no way she would willingly leave the chateau with this stranger.

Any relief she had momentarily felt to be out of Nanny Beth's clutches had drained from her mind.

"Perhaps you should interrupt him from his busy day to release a charge from his care," the gentleman said. "Go and find the headmaster if you don't believe we have spoken about this matter in depth."

Nanny Beth folded the letter with shaking hands, offering it back to the gentleman and turning to Etta. "Do you know this gentleman?"

Etta shook her head. "I have never seen him before today."

"Your father insisted we marry. The document includes his signature," the man said. "Have a second look."

"My father is dead! Same as you will be if you don't leave this instant!" Etta's top lip curled as she threatened him to get out of Ashby. He did not belong here. Didn't Nanny Beth recognize that? Where were the other nannies and papas? With all the commotion, where was her papa, Philip?

"Silence, child!" Nanny Beth swatted Etta's bottom.

With the dress being far too short and scandalous, the bloomers were the only level of protection against her raw backside. The spanking still hurt profusely.

"I assure you that I have spoken in length with your headmaster. He assured me that my paperwork is in order, but if you cannot get him down here at once, I can bring in my lawyer and make this a much more public matter."

"No. That will not be necessary. Etta, you are to go with Mr. Maddock."

Etta's eyes widened and she shook her head. "Please, you cannot do this!" She took several tentative steps back, though where would she run to? How far would she get without making a scene and only causing more trouble. Did Papa really want her gone?

"Grab your belongings at once," Mr. Maddock said.

Etta had nothing. The clothes she'd come to Ashby with had been taken away. Did they store the dress for safe keeping, or toss it into a furnace?

"She is ready as she is," Nanny Beth said. Her hands gripped Etta's shoulders, pushing her toward the stranger. "Go with your new papa."

Mr. Maddock cleared his throat. "I am not her papa. I am her betrothed." He snatched Etta's hand and led her down the hall and through the doors that led outside.

"Who did this?" Etta asked, trying to yank her hand from Mr. Maddock's. Had it been Papa Philip's doing, or her Uncle Jack's?

"The only one doing anything is you, Henrietta. I suggest you come with me or face my belt the moment we get into the carriage."

Etta shut her mouth. It seemed Papa Philip had perhaps been the one to send her away. Wordlessly, she followed the gentleman to his carriage. The sky had grown dark and her stomach rumbled from having missed dinner.

He opened and shut the coach door for her, sitting down opposite her in the carriage.

She stared out of the window, at the darkness of night. "Where are we going?" Etta asked.

"To my home," he answered, not elaborating any further.

"Mr. Maddock. Do you have a first name? If we are to be wed, I think I should know what it is."

He nodded. "Yes. It is Thomas." The horses inched forward, moving the carriage along with them through the open, wrought-iron gates out of Ashby's property. "You will come home with me and we shall be wed at once. I need a mother to my two girls, and you seem quite capable, once we get you out of that hideous dress. You are a grown woman and you will be expected to dress and behave as such."

Etta's eyes welled, and she felt grateful for the lack of moonlight to show her features. Already she missed the chateau—since her father had passed away, it was the closest thing to a home she had found. Had she been such a terrible little that Papa Philip had sent her away to marry the first man available? "You have two children?" she repeated.

"Yes. From my first wife, who died of consumption."

Etta relaxed. At least she had not been murdered. Perhaps Thomas was a good man. "I am sorry about your wife."

"As am I, but it was many years ago."

"I am to become a mother?" Etta asked. She assumed that was why he wanted to marry her, to bring structure to the two girls living under his roof, his children.

"You will eventually bear children, but my main concerns are the two brats eating all my food and their lack of discipline. I expect you to keep them in line."

"You desire me to be their nanny?" Etta wished she could escape the carriage, but how far would she get? If the paper was indeed true, then she was betrothed to Thomas Maddock and her choices were eliminated.

"I expect you to cuddle the children, read them bedtime stories, and pay them the proper attention they need to grow into young ladies. The governess will be providing them with an education, and the nanny will be tending to the children's daily needs."

Her responsibilities did not sound terrible, though what did she know of helping raise children? She had none of her own and the time she had spent looking after her dying father, did not seem like it would have provided her with enough useful knowledge.

"Rest," Thomas said. "There will be plenty to do upon our arrival."

Etta shut her eyes but could not relax on the ride to Thomas's home. Her stomach ached with regret, already missing Philip far more than she should have. He'd got to her, made her feel something for him in a way she had never imagined possible. Etta refused to cry, biting down on her tongue, forcing herself to concentrate on the small sharp stab of pain instead of the raw tugging at her heart. Bitterness and anger itched in her hands, forcing her fists to ball at her sides. Philip had been nowhere to be found, selling her to the nearest buyer so that he wouldn't have to look upon her ever again. She found it difficult to sleep, and tossed between a restless slumber and sadness plaguing her dreams.

SIXTEEN

PHILIP HAD NOT TUCKED Etta into bed, though he had wanted to. He had more trivial matters to attend to, and disciplining Mae was at the top of his agenda. After careful consideration, he had decided that removing her from the littles' wing had not been enough. She needed a healthy reminder to keep her in line at his school.

"I am displeased, Mae." He did not bother to address her by her previous title of nanny. She had been stripped of that responsibility, and would have to earn respect from him once again.

"I am sorry, Headmaster Philip," Mae said, apologetically. "I do not know what came over me."

"I do." His jaw remained tight, his fists at his sides. "You decided to take advantage of my little Etta." He walked toward the desk and opened the top drawer, revealing several disciplinary elements that were used on the girls at the chateau.

"She is a grown woman who consented to what happened," Mae said, excusing her behavior and her actions.

"In our care, she did not have the ability to consent. She is to be treated as a little at all times, and you took advantage of that with *my* Etta." He'd grown so fond of her in such a short time. "You are to lower your drawers and bare your bottom."

"Excuse me?" Mae's voice trembled.

"You heard me." Philip was not going to let this go without ample punishment. He'd do the same to a little who took advantage of a nanny or papa. No one was above the rules of Ashby.

Mae turned around, her back to him as she lowered her drawers to her ankles. She reached for the hem of her dress, lifting it to reveal her porcelain freckled bottom. The skin appeared smooth to the touch, without any marks or traces of recent spankings as far as Philip could tell.

"Lean forward onto the desk and push your bottom out and up."

"Mr. Hartley," she said, her voice quivering as she shook.

"It is Headmaster Hartley," he corrected her. Grabbing the nearby ruler, he smacked her nether cheeks. "Hurry up. I do not have all day!" He was not pleased with how long it seemed to be taking her to follow his instructions.

Mae stood with her legs a couple of inches apart. She leaned forward, pressing her breasts against the table.

"Legs further apart," Philip ordered. He landed another blow with the ruler to both buttocks, making her jump. Did she enjoy his attention? He had not done it to pleasure her, but he was getting quite an eyeful of her glistening quim as she spread her legs.

The pink pucker on her bottom was a gorgeous sight, and if she'd been his or one of the littles, he'd have plugged it after her discipline.

"A little further." He nudged her thighs with the ruler and she spread them apart, her hands finding the edge of the desk, gripping it. "Good." He traded the ruler for the cane, wanting to ensure each blow landed exactly as he directed it. "You will receive fifteen strokes for your behavior."

Mae gasped. "I would never do that many on a little."

"Complain and I shall make it twenty," Philip said. He whipped the cane through the air, smacking her bottom, leaving a red welt that matched her hair. "Count for me."

"One."

Her hips bucked and body jumped as he swatted her rear. "Push your bottom out and up," he said, reminding her of the position he wanted her in. It gave him the perfect glimpse of her slick pussy and her growing welts as he landed the cane on her again.

"Two."

Philip would have felt bad for caning Mae fifteen times, but she'd been a nanny since he opened Ashby. This may have been her first offense, but he was going to see to it that it would be her last. She would have her job with the finishing school and a sore bottom to remind her not to make the same mistake ever again.

The cane came down again and Mae no longer held her tongue. "I am sorry," she whimpered as tears puddled before her. Shaking, her bottom swelled with each welt.

"What number?" Philip asked. "Or shall I have you start from the beginning?"

"Three!" she cried out. "Please, no more."

"I have only given you three strokes. I assure you that your bottom can handle plenty more."

Her fingers clenched the edge of the wooden table and her toes pushed her feet up, giving him the perfect view as he released the cane again and again.

"Four. Five." She winced, a hiss slipping past her lips. "Please, no more!"

Philip ignored her pleas and continued whipping his wrist, landing blow after blow with the cane to her rear.

"Six. Seven." Her body squirmed with each stroke, her hips shifting and her toes lifting her higher.

Welts covered her cheeks and Philip landed several additional blows lower down, knowing the effect they would have on her.

Her whimpers turned to cries of pain.

"Count!" he ordered.

"That was ten."

He forgave her for not speaking the numbers eight and nine aloud. She had been preoccupied with the cane to her bottom. "Should I continue?"

"Please, no," Mae sobbed, her body shaking as he let the cane land on her bottom.

"Eleven," Philip said, counting for her. "I find no pleasure in caning you for your behavior." He wanted it clear that she may have been disciplined, but he sought no enjoyment from it. Unlike putting Etta over his lap and spanking her, which aroused him greatly, his affection for Mae was strictly platonic. His lesson here was to keep her from making the same mistake again, as well as to ensure that she understood that there would be consequences for such actions.

Mae let go of the table and reached behind her, trying to shield her bottom from any further lashings. "Please. I shall take the rest of my allotment tomorrow."

"That is not how it works," Philip said. Her bottom matched the color of burgundy and though he knew she would find it impossible to sit comfortably for presumably a week, it was much deserved. Another swat landed on her rear, this one slightly higher on her bottom. "Twelve."

He continued counting with each blow, ignoring the sounds of her whimpers and tears. Her bottom swelled and he'd covered every ounce of her perfectly freckled skin with welts from the cane, finally reaching fifteen.

As he put the cane away, Mae did not move from her position against the table.

"Get up. Your punishment is complete. Unless you want to embrace the paddle tonight, as well?" he asked.

Mae released her hold on the table, pushing herself to stand, the hem of her dress falling down around her legs. She did not lift the bloomers, stepping out of them instead. "I am sorry for taking advantage of little Etta. It will not happen again. Thank you for my punishment," she said.

Philip nodded his acceptance. She had answered exactly as he'd expect any one of his littles to respond after a session of discipline.

"You are forgiven." Though he was not pleased with what she had done, Etta was no worse for wear. He placed the ruler back into the drawer, with the paddle and cane at its side.

"Thank you."

"I expect you to work with the girls at our finishing school, remind them that they do not want a red bottom like the one you are wearing right now. If you were a little, I would have you stand in the playroom with your dress up, letting all the others see the evidence of your discipline." He had no reason to further embarrass her. The discipline and lesson had been completed.

Philip stepped out from her office and headed through the halls of the finishing school toward the door that led to his littles' establishment. Retrieving the key attached to his pocket watch, he flipped it open to see the hour. It was long past Etta's bedtime. He hoped Nanny Beth had been able to put Etta into bed without too much trouble. Tomorrow he'd get a report of her behavior and hopefully would not have to instill too much additional discipline.

SEVENTEEN

"WE HAVE ARRIVED," Thomas said, his voice stirring Etta from her slumber.

Unlike Philip, who had carried Etta inside and put her to bed, Thomas showed no indication of offering any help or gentlemanly behavior. Why was he pursuing her hand in marriage? Was it solely her dowry he was after? She would have to find out, but tonight she needed rest.

Rubbing the sleep from her eyes, she stumbled from the carriage, tripping over her feet. Thomas grabbed her arm, catching her before she had time to land face-first in the dirt.

"Careful. There is not much light out here during a new moon," Thomas said. The coachman lit a candle and offered it to Thomas. "Come," he directed, taking her hand as he led her up the dark steps and inside his home.

Etta had not got a good look at the house in the dark but it appeared large in scale, much like the chateau, or how she saw it upon leaving. She had not been awake when she had arrived and had been made to stay within specific quarters, but based on the limited knowledge, she assumed it to be much larger in size.

Thomas dropped her hand and used the candle to light the lantern, casting a warm glow to the foyer, basking it in shadows. There wasn't much to see with all the doors closed for the night, as the two stood in the hall, likely to keep the chill down and the rooms upstairs warm. Etta wrapped her arms around herself, still feeling quite cool inside. The floorboards were wooden and as she stepped further inside, her heels clicked against them. She attempted to tread more lightly and softly, not wanting to wake his sleeping children. The lamplight stretched only as far as the stairs, and the banister had been carved most delicately, with a beautiful design of swirls and unusual patterns in the wood that she found mesmerizing. The house smelled pleasant, like the embers of a nearby fire burning, but she did not see any hearth or feel its much needed heat. Perhaps it was keeping the nanny or maid's quarters warm.

"You have a lovely home," Etta said, trying to be both polite and quiet.

"Thank you. It will be your home soon, too," Thomas said. "Come. I shall show you to your room."

Etta breathed a sigh of relief, grateful he had not mentioned 'their' room. She'd have a place of her own to sleep, which was much needed.

"I shall have Nanny Joan fetch you my late wife's gowns from the attic tomorrow. Perhaps you will find something more appropriate to wear in the armoire for tonight." He glanced Etta over, obviously not impressed by the dress.

She had not been pleased with the bright pink dress that seemed appropriate for a six-year-old, either. "Thank you." She tried to be as polite as possible, unsure about her place or how long she'd be staying with Thomas Maddock. Would he grow tired of her just as Philip had? Or perhaps he would decide that she would stay with him indefinitely, they would marry, and she would raise his children and have even more of their own.

Etta had not spent any time thinking about a family much beyond a husband. She had been so focused on pleasing Philip recently, and looking after her father before that, she had forgotten about the world's expectations of her as a woman. For the briefest of moments, she had felt wonderful with Philip; loved, cherished, and innocent like a child. Those days were over. Etta felt as if they'd abandoned her, the precious and easy life slipping away, disappearing into a vat of nothingness.

He led her to a bedroom at the top of the stairwell. Paintings of the children hung in the hall. What other displays of art were hidden behind the doors downstairs? Perhaps there was something about Thomas she could find endearing. Tomorrow, when the mood struck, she would ask him about his favorite painters and artists. Was it possible that he had a painting of her father's hanging in his study or dining room? What she would give to glimpse a work of his art every day, to feel right at home in this new place.

"My maids should have left you a few nightgowns in the armoire," Thomas said.

Etta stepped inside the bedroom, taking it all in. The bedroom was quaint. The oversized mattress was dressed in a dark gray quilt, and in the corner of the room nestled a cherry armoire for her things, not that she had anything but the dress she wore. Perhaps she should have been grateful the room hadn't been decorated as a nursery like Ashby. However, the walls were covered with white and gray stripes, a decadent wallpaper that had been freshly applied, with an odd sheen and texture that Etta wanted to run her fingers against, certain she could feel it as well as see the design. She had never seen anything quite like it.

Stalking across the room, Thomas opened the doors of the armoire to reveal half a dozen dresses, some night attire, and other day gowns to wear.

At least she had an array of clothes to choose from that weren't immature and appropriate only for a young child. Had her uncle saved the gowns for the day she was to wed? Perhaps he would bring the dresses to her soon. Wearing a dead woman's clothes felt highly inappropriate.

"Thank you. You have been exceptionally kind." Etta wanted Thomas to know she appreciated the gesture. If this was to be her life, she would do her best to make the most of it.

"Of course. They were just gathering dust anyway." He left the armoire open. "Change for bed and then meet me across the hall in my room."

"Your room?" she asked, her stomach a bundle of nerves. What was he expecting of her? She cast her eyes briefly to the windowsill. It was much too high for her to make an escape. Besides, where would she go? Thomas hadn't done anything to offend her. She needed to calm down.

"I shall have the cook bring up a tray of desserts for us to nibble on while we get better acquainted with one another. I assume the nap you had on our way to the estate did tide you over?" Thomas asked.

Etta did not want to lie. She was still tired, but he was probably right. She would not sleep even if she lay in bed. When her head hit the pillow, she would be awake as day. "The rest was helpful. Thank you," she said.

"Good. Come as soon as you get out of that dreadful attire," he said, gesturing toward the pink dress. "It is horrific. Whoever put you in that should be hanged."

She clamped her mouth shut, deciding not to confess that she had dressed herself. Yes, it was bright and blinding, but it had been far better than the other clothes in the wardrobe that had been provided for Etta to wear.

Thomas headed for the door. "I shall leave my room open so you will be able to find me." He stepped out of her room and shut the door behind him.

Etta fumbled through the half dozen dresses that had been previously worn by Thomas's deceased wife. Would it not be odd for him to see Etta in the same clothes? Was he perhaps trying to replace his late wife with her? She had no money, the estate and finances were all tied up with her Uncle Jack. He was supposed to be saving her gowns for when she married. Had he kept his word, or would she be forced to beg a few shillings from Thomas for dresses of her own?

She settled on a white cotton gown that seemed thick enough not to reveal her nipples. What would Thomas think if he saw her naked? Her bottom still held a hint of blush from her spankings and her quim was free of any and all hair, thanks to the people at the chateau insisting she be raised and cared for as a little.

Would Thomas understand what she had gone through or think them all mad? If Philip had a hand in this arrangement of marriage, then certainly Thomas must have an inkling of what the chateau was all about. Except his look of disgust upon seeing her in that pink dress made her question everything she had learned since she arrived at Ashby.

Etta removed the gown from the hanger and disrobed as quickly as possible, not wanting to leave Thomas unattended for too long. She would have to discuss his expectations and desires. Did he wish a wife, or solely a mother to his two girls? He had shown no hint of affection toward her, which was fine with Etta. Perhaps if he was expecting a mother and nothing more, then she could get something that she desired in return. An exchange of services or goods, but what did she want?

Thomas seemed nice enough, offering Etta her own room and a small but simple wardrobe. She would insist that Uncle Jack bring her gowns. Even if she did not have the power to make such a request, Thomas could do it for her. Surely he'd be thrilled with the dresses from her time with her father, and prefer them to the gowns of his late wife.

She slipped the dress on over her head and fastened the laces at the sides, which made the gown easier to put on herself. Had his wife preferred not to be doted on? Etta headed out from the bedroom and down the hall. A lantern hung along the way, making it easy to see as she wandered toward the open bedroom.

"May I come in?" Etta asked, trying to be as polite as possible. It felt strange to be not only in this man's home, but in his bedroom. Not even at Ashby had she set foot in her papa's bedroom. Had he even had a room to stay in at night? It seemed he was always there, since he was the headmaster.

"Please, do." Thomas gestured toward the small sitting space set up in his room with a couch and table. "Have a seat."

The walls of his bedroom matched hers with the same decorative wallpaper. The biggest difference, aside from his room being twice as large, were the two paintings that hung on the walls. Etta desired to stare at them every night before falling asleep, both were tranquil and serene scenes that had been obviously painted by two different artists. Just above the incredibly large mattress sat the painting of an afternoon landscape of a prairie of wildflowers. Opposite the window, a second painting, much more abstract and grander in size, was affixed to the wall. Both paintings were quite marvelous. Were the wildflowers painted from a real place? She had never seen such beauty, and yet she wanted to go and visit it at once.

Thomas had not changed out of his clothes and Etta felt underdressed in her nightgown. "This is highly inappropriate," she stammered. "We may be betrothed, but we are not married."

A smile softened his features. "I assure you, Henrietta, that your virginity will remain intact until our wedding night."

Her cheeks blushed. "I prefer to be called Etta," she said, correcting him.

"Of course you do. Your Uncle Jack mentioned you had a bit of a temper and a mouth on you."

"You know my uncle?" Etta ignored the comment referring to her behavior. Her Uncle Jack barely knew her, and the few minutes he had spent with her were not enough for him to be able to fairly make any judgments about her as a person.

"Not personally. I knew your father. He suggested the arrangement after my wife passed."

Perhaps that explained the art and paintings affixed to his walls. His having known her father put her more at ease with Thomas. "Oh." Etta had no idea her father had found her a suitable husband. "When was this?" she asked.

"You were sixteen at the time. I suggested we meet, but he insisted to wait until after a year of mourning. My wife had just passed and he had been right, I needed a year to reflect and adjust."

Etta knew what had happened then. Her father's sickness had taken more of him away from her. He had probably forgotten he'd even promised her hand to anyone. "Why wasn't the lawyer notified?" Surely he'd have held the paperwork that divulged her father's wishes.

"A very good question indeed." Thomas reached for the tea and poured them each a cup. "How do you take your tea?"

"Without sugar," she said, and lifted the fine porcelain to her lips. The steam swirled around her chin before she opened her mouth, taking a brief taste of the piping hot liquid. It burned on its way down. Her chest felt hot and uncomfortable. Placing the cup back down on the table, the roof of her mouth burned and she knew it would feel unpleasant for the next few days. She'd have to be more careful. Philip would have certainly scolded her.

"Hot isn't it?" Thomas asked, holding his own cup in his hands, but waiting for the liquid to cool. "I know you have been dragged away from your education, but I do not believe a finishing school will teach you anything you need to know as my wife." He blew on the tea, the steam wafting to the side momentarily as he took a sip. Thomas did not so much as flinch. How did he do that? Drink such a hot liquid and not burn his mouth or throat?

"I see," Etta said, though she did not quite see what it was that Thomas wanted. "Are you desiring solely a mother for your children, or a wife as well?" She needed to know what his expectations were.

"That is quite a loaded question," Thomas said, his dark gaze locked on her. "Your father asked me to look after you, marry you, and bestow upon you the Maddock name. You will be my wife, Etta."

At least he respected her enough to call her by the name she desired. "How did you know where to find me?" Etta asked.

"I may not have known your uncle personally, but I did come upon him after I spoke with your father's estate attorney. It turns out he had sole custody of you and your dowry. He has released you into my care and once we are wed, the dowry and half the estate is mine."

"Half the estate?" Etta asked, not understanding. "What about the other half?"

"Your Uncle Jack was not so quick to part with you or your money. Surprising, since I hear he sent you away on the first night on which you arrived at his home. The past does not matter, Etta. I am your future. You will be my wife, the mother of my children, and make me happy."

Etta did not feel quite pleased with the arrangement but there were far worse situations to be in. Thomas seemed nice, his home pleasant, and it felt as though he wanted her there with him. She reached for her tea, taking another sip. The liquid had not had enough time to cool and again burned her lips. "Christ," she muttered under her breath, putting the cup on the table.

Thomas narrowed his eyes. "What was that?"

"Forgive me, sir. I continue to burn myself. I find I am not used to tea so hot and fresh," she said, trying to apologize.

"Proper ladies do not use such vulgar, blasphemous and disrespectful language in this home."

"I am sorry," Etta said again.

"That is not enough. Stand up this instant." He stared at her, waiting for her to follow his order.

Etta slowly stood up, gazing down at him fearfully.

"Take off your dress. You will be soundly thrashed for the words that slipped from that tongue of yours.

Be glad I am not cleaning your mouth out with soap. Luckily for you, I need the maid to fetch some, but if she were on duty at this hour, I would be shoving a bar in your mouth."

Etta wished more than anything she'd have put those stupid bloomers back on. Embarrassed, she lifted the gown up off her body, letting it hit the floor.

Thomas stood and walked over toward the bed. Sitting atop the dresser was a strip of black leather, looped over itself. "Over my knees," he said, ordering her down onto his lap as he sat on the edge of the mattress.

"What is that?"

"A strap. This is what you will get to your backside for disobeying the rules of the house."

She swallowed nervously, knowing what was to come. She had been spanked enough times now to know it would not be pleasant, though it had never been with a strap. It looked a bit like a belt, though shorter, and with less chance of landing anywhere but its intended destination.

Etta rested her stomach over his lap, her breasts brushing against his pants. He had the perfect view of her taut cheeks.

"I suggest you relax. Clenching only makes the pain worse. Spread your legs further apart," he commanded.

Etta separated her legs until they were a hands-width apart.

"More."

She guided her legs further and felt her quim open. A cool rush of air seeped toward the heat of her thighs. She buried her head downward, refusing to show her face. This was humiliating! Was this how he intended to discipline her after they were married?

The strap came down without warning, causing Etta to jump and flinch. Her hips lifted off his waist and she yelped in protest.

"Enough!" He did not seem pleased by her outburst. "You will wake the girls."

Good. Then maybe he would be forced to stop. She did not dare ask how many swats she'd get to her rear.

The strap came down again, this time between her cheeks, and with her legs separated, she could have sworn it grazed her pink pucker, forcing another whimper from her lips. He did not soften any blows by rubbing her bottom, or soothe her with any consoling words.

She knew this was discipline but it felt harsher, stricter than she was used to. Perhaps it was because she'd only said a bad word, and he was using a strap that was causing far more pain than a simple spanking with his hand would have. She had not realized how much more she preferred Nanny Mae's firm palm to anything else that landed on her bottom.

Thomas let the strap smack her arse again. A new welt blossomed on her backside, she felt certain that the blistering would take weeks to go away. The pain radiated deep below the surface of skin.

"I am sorry," she whispered. Tears did not come but the pain certainly grew with each stroke of the strap. He covered her plush cheeks, just below her bottom and two more swats to the top of her roundness. Thomas was certainly making sure to leave no area white for her lesson on proper language in his home.

Etta lost count of the number of strokes she endured with the strap. Tears finally came and soaked his pants, though Thomas made no mention of it. When he finished, he dropped the implement onto the bed.

"Stand up, look at me," he said, giving her commands. She had no choice but to follow them, afraid he'd continue spanking her raw bottom otherwise.

Etta met his stare, her eyes must have been red and swollen from crying.

"After every punishment, you will show your remorse by baring every bit of flesh for an hour. Anyone who walks in will see what you have done. They'll be witness to your swollen bottom. This is how you will atone for your sins."

She swallowed nervously. "What if your children walk in?"

"Then what better a lesson for them to learn than to see what happens when they do not obey their husband," Thomas said. "If you are shy in regards to your body, then I expect you will not make the same mistake ever again."

She reached to cover her breasts but he captured her hands in his. "Do not hide yourself from me or anyone else on this estate. Is that understood?"

"Yes, sir."

"Now go and stand with your nose in the corner and your hands resting on the top of your head."

She did as he ordered without saying another word.

EIGHTEEN

REGRETTING that he'd missed reading Etta a story last night before bed, Philip checked in on the nursery, not finding any sign of Etta. Her bed was made, the room quiet and dark.

Perhaps she was with the littles in the playroom. It was far too late for her to still be eating breakfast. Nanny Beth would have got Etta up early and made sure she was finished with her meal and bath before ten. It was nearing eleven, and he had not seen any sign of her. The littles' wing in Ashby was not that big.

Heading toward the playroom, he glanced through the glass window. He caught sight of Gracie and

Leda playing quietly together. Where the blazes was his little Etta?

Nanny Beth sat with Nanny Vivian, chatting together in the corner by the door. Why was Nanny Beth not with Etta? His head spun with rage. Yes, he'd been mistaken about Nanny Mae and had been a fool to trust her, but Nanny Beth had given him no reason to doubt her. Elizabeth had done an amazing job with the young ladies at the finishing school. Why would her behavior have changed overnight?

Demanding an answer, Philip forced the door open and entered like a storm at sea. "Where is Etta?" He did not wait for her to answer as he stalked up to Nanny Beth. Leda and Gracie were coloring. The girls' heads shot up, their hands pausing over the paper with wide curious eyes.

Perhaps it was best to keep this between the adults. "Outside. Now." He headed for the door, his footsteps heavy on the carpeting as he held it open for Nanny Beth. The moment she stepped out, he let the door slam shut behind her, making it known to all that he was furious.

"Where is Etta?"

"Her papa came to retrieve her last night," Nanny Beth said.

"What?" Philip shook his head. Had he misheard the woman? "*I* am her papa. What are you talking about? Who came to the chateau?" His heart skipped a beat and sweat beaded on his brow. Who would come and kidnap his little girl?

Nanny Beth took a tentative step backwards, concern dawning on her face. "Oh dear. I do not remember the gentleman's name. He arrived with a carriage and had the paperwork that said that Miss Etta was to wed him. It was all in order. He even insisted he had spoken with you and that I was to release her into his care."

"How could you let a stranger take *my* little Etta!" Philip's fists balled at his sides in rage as he stepped closer to Nanny Beth, demanding to know the truth. Had Etta desired to leave the chateau? She'd been doing well with her training, but there had been some setbacks recently.

"I am so sorry, Headmaster Philip." Beth's voice trembled and she wrung her hands together in front of her.

"Sorry is not enough! It does not bring my Etta back!" How could she have blindly gone with a stranger? Had no one else heard the commotion and come to see what was going on? "Did she ask to leave with him?" he went on. Could she have betrayed him by asking a staff member to send a message to someone to help aid in her escape? Would she be so selfish and insolent to do such a thing?

"N-no," Nanny Beth stammered, shaking her head. "Etta was not pleased to go with the gentleman." Her entire body shook in fear and her eyes glistened with tears. "I am so sorry, Headmaster Philip. Please, do not fire me. I need this job, sir. I have a daughter at home and my husband died last December. This is the only way I am able to put food on the table and keep us from living on the street." She continued to ramble and Philip let her, his mind racing about all the terrible things that could be happening to his Etta. "I swear, if I'd had any inkling that he did not belong, I would have come and found you at once. The gentleman kept insisting that he had spoken with you and that he would bring his lawyers here if I did not release her into his custody. I know what that would do to you and this school, and the reputation you have built. I was only trying to help ward off further attention."

Philip tried to ignore the sound of her pleas. He had to look after *his* little one. She was out there, alone with a stranger who seemed to have no respect for the system or authority. What kind of gentleman would swoop in and threaten to expose the chateau by bringing a lawyer into the discussions, unless he was trouble? Which meant Etta was in danger.

The hall spun and sweat coated his skin. He felt as though he might be sick as his heart beat in his chest at an unprecedented pace. Philip would not let anything happen to Etta. "What am I supposed to do, Beth?" he asked. How was he going to find his little love? She was gone, swept off by a stranger with a slip of paper. His anger needed not be directed at Nanny Beth. She had only done what she thought was right, and best for Etta and for the school. Slowly he had to come to terms with what she had done. It had not been to spite him.

"I am sorry, Headmaster Philip. I do not know how to find her. Perhaps if the gentleman spoke the truth and was her betrothed, then her family would know how to find her."

The pit that had formed in his stomach did not vanish but his anger slowly dissipated. Who would have had the rare stones to steal Etta from the chateau, except for Jack Waters? Had someone come to him with a better offer of marriage to his niece? One that did not involve the cost of her education, perchance?

His ears reddened and his neck flushed as though covered with a rash as anger surged through him a second time in just a few short minutes. "By any chance was the gentleman's name Jack Waters?" he asked. Could Etta's uncle have arrived at the chateau and decided against keeping her enrolled?

"No. That was not it, although the name Waters is familiar. Is that Miss Etta's name?" Nanny Beth asked.

"Yes. Henrietta Waters."

"Right!" Beth said, her eyes lighting up. "That was the name on the sheet."

It did little good for her to remember Etta's given name. Had she had an inkling of the man's name, that would have been helpful. "Did he happen to express where he was taking her?" Philip asked again.

"No. I am sorry. If they were betrothed, then I assume he was bringing her back home with him."

Philip could have deduced that much himself. He let out an anxious breath, his hands visibly shaking, though he hoped Nanny Beth had not noticed. "I need to spend some time away from the chateau. Do you think you might be able to look after the littles while I am gone? Specifically, little Gracie. She will need your guidance." He'd only assigned Etta to Nanny Beth but without Nanny Mae, Gracie needed a caring yet firm hand, and Nanny Vivian was looking after little Leda. He did not dare think what would happen between them while he was away. He would have to keep his travel plans a secret from the littles. If they had any idea that only the nannies and their papas were in charge, the place could get turned upside down.

"Of course," Nanny Beth said. "I am sorry about Etta. I had no idea the gentleman was not her papa."

How could she have known? She had been assigned to the finishing school until just yesterday. She did not know who visited, who the girls were betrothed to, and what was expected of the littles. Philip could only blame himself for what had happened. It made him realize that anyone could enter the chateau and take the girls at whim. Not only did he need to find Etta, but he would have to strengthen the security at Ashby. This type of situation must never happen again.

NINETEEN

ETTA HAD BEEN HUMILIATED the previous night. After having had the strap applied repeatedly to her bottom, she had been forced to stand completely nude in Thomas's room in the corner until he'd told her to go to bed. Thankfully, the children had not woken, but two other visitors had come by his room. Etta had paid little attention to their names or their positions. The embarrassment had been far too much. They'd been respectful enough not to make any comments. Had they seen this display of power before? Thomas had been married previously. Had his wife truly died, or had she felt unable to take it and run away? Etta did not want to consider what kind of a mother would abandon her children.

"Good morning," a soft small voice greeted her.

Etta rolled onto her side, the gown riding up her thighs as the blankets curled around her. Her bottom still felt sore but she had kept her weight off it while sleeping and would make as many attempts to avoid sitting on it today as well.

Opening her eyes, she found herself staring at a child not more than five or six, with hair as dark as ink and eyes just like her father's. "Hello," Etta said, wondering what the child's name was.

"Hello." The young girl smiled ruefully at Etta.

"Come, Sophia!" a woman scolded the young girl. "I am so sorry, miss."

"It is all right," Etta said, sitting up in bed. She grimaced the moment her bottom hit the mattress. Jumping from the bed, she headed for the armoire, as if that had been her intention all along, to start her day.

Sophia smiled. Did she know what was going on? Etta had not met her last night, but that did not mean she had not heard about it, either.

"I am Nanny Joan, though it seems I might not be around here much longer," the woman said.

"What? Why would you say that?" Etta spun around on her feet, confused.

"Because the children have you now," Nanny Joan said.

Etta shook her head. No. Thomas had never mentioned anything about being their nanny. In fact, he had made it clear that they had a nanny and governess already.

"Do not leave us, Nanny Joan," Sophia said, clinging to the woman's arms.

Etta bent down to face the young girl. "Your Nanny Joan is not going anywhere. All right? I promise you, she will be here as long as she would like to be." Though she knew she had no say in what happened in the Maddock household, she also did not want to scare the child into hating her already. If Thomas spoke about dismissing Nanny Joan, then Etta would step in and speak her mind. She hoped that did not happen anytime soon. Her bottom was still sore from last night, and would be for quite some time.

Sophia watched Etta carefully before relinquishing her tight grasp on Nanny Joan. "Will you come play with me?"

Nanny Joan patted Sophia's back. "How about we let this nice woman get dressed first?"

"I'm Etta," she said, introducing herself. "It is short for Henrietta."

"All right," Sophia said, pouting as Nanny Joan guided her out of the room by her shoulders.

"It is nice to meet you, Etta," Nanny Joan said as she closed the door behind her, leaving the young woman in peace.

Etta walked toward the armoire. What could she wear? The dresses may have only been a few years old, sitting in a closet for safe keeping, but they were not her style; with sequins and silk, far too fancy for an ordinary afternoon. Though, in truth, nothing about Etta's life was typical lately. She had no idea what to expect from Thomas, let alone whether Philip even cared that she had left. Had he been angry when he discovered she had gone missing? She had thought Philip had sent her away, but now that she knew that hadn't been the case, she felt bad about going without saying goodbye. Not that Thomas had afforded her that luxury.

She removed the cotton nightgown and changed into a dark red dress that matched the color of her bottom. Since the welts had had only minimal time to heal, they still hurt immensely as the fabric grazed her skin. Etta did not bother with undergarments, for it felt far more comfortable with nothing underneath after the lashing she'd had for speaking inappropriately. Perhaps if she said nothing to Thomas from now on, it would keep her out of further trouble.

Stepping out from the bedroom, Etta wandered the hall and down the stairs, following the sounds of young children laughing. Would this be her life from now on, caring for Thomas' two girls? It did not sound too terrible, but it was not what she wanted. She missed the chateau and everything it offered. Being cared for and loved had been a wonderful feeling; even with the discipline that had followed. With Thomas, she had the discipline but nothing that made her feel warm and adored, not like with Philip and the nannies.

"Hello, girls," Etta said as she entered the playroom.

Sophia's smile grew with her happiness. "Miss Etta!"

"It is just Etta." She did not want the children to be so formal around her. "I met Sophia upstairs." Etta walked toward the girl who was a bit taller than Sophia, with hair just as dark and matching dark brown eyes. "What is your name?"

The young girl did not answer. She spun around on the floor with her doll, intentionally ignoring Etta.

"She is Mary," Nanny Joan said. "I am sorry about that. Mary is usually so much better behaved. It has been hard after her mother passed away. She is not very accepting of her father's guests."

"Guests?" Did Nanny Joan mean that Etta was not the first woman he had brought into his home? How many others had he considered marrying? What had happened? Had the children driven them off? "Thomas and I are betrothed," Etta added, pointedly.

"My apologies," Nanny Joan said. "I am sure Mary will come around when she realizes you are to be her mother."

Etta could not even remember her own mother. Her father had never been able to afford a nanny or anyone else to care for his daughter.

Heavy footsteps traveled through the hall and into the playroom. "Good," Thomas said. "I have been looking for you this morning, Etta. Come join me for breakfast." It was not a question, but a demand.

"Yes, of course." Etta followed Thomas from the playroom. She glanced back over her shoulder as Mary spun around and stuck her tongue out at her. That child would be difficult indeed. She did not wish to think about the other women who had been chased away by two rambunctious children, though Sophia seemed quite polite and easy to attend to.

"How are you liking the estate thus far?" Thomas asked.

"Your home is quite lovely, as are your daughters."

A smile grazed his features. "I look forward to fathering more children with you." His hand came to rest atop her stomach.

Etta's belly flipped. She had not even thought about children. It would be expected of her to lie in bed with him and produce babies, but she still found the idea repulsive. "I do not know," she stammered.

"You will give me at least three more children. I need a boy to carry on the Maddock name," Thomas informed her.

"Three children?" Etta spat out. He expected five children to run around the estate without incident? It seemed Nanny Joan had enough with just the two girls, keeping her hands plenty full.

"Unless you would like five more?" Thomas said. "I would be quite happy to renegotiate our terms."

Had he not considered the cost of raising so many young children, or was money no object for Thomas? Etta knew her dowry would go to him and it seemed that he'd also acquire some of the funds from the sale of her childhood home.

"Three more children is sufficient," she said, walking alongside him as she followed Thomas into the dining room. The room was rectangular in shape, which matched the large rectangle mahogany table situated several meters inside. A dozen wooden chairs with high backs and intricate carvings matched the table. Sunlight poured in through the window, making the cream colored walls a warm yellow, as the dark gray curtains had been pulled to the side. Sitting on the table was an assortment of breads, fruits, cheeses, and juices. Her mouth watered and stomach rumbled at the sight of such a feast. It all smelled delicious.

"Glad we have that settled." Thomas pulled out the chair and Etta headed over to take a seat, only to see him sit himself down.

She paused, a confused look on her face, before dragging the heavy wooden chair several steps back. Etta sat down, hiding the discomfort of her raw bottom, and scooted herself in, the chair squeaking as it dragged across the floor.

Thomas seemed distracted, dishing out food onto his plate, apparently not even noticing his lack of manners. Was this how he always behaved? If so, then maybe it explained Mary's cold shoulder. She had blatantly learned it from somewhere.

"Help yourself," Thomas said, gesturing toward the trays on the table. He dug in, hungrily devouring his meal. Glancing up after several minutes, his food nearly finished, he examined Etta. "Tell me about your time at Ashby. What were you doing at the

Ashby Chateau? Teaching young girls, or taking lessons for yourself?" He sipped his tea, his eyes never leaving hers.

Etta knew lying was a terrible idea, but she could not reveal to him the truth about what had been expected of her at Ashby. He would not understand. It had been kept a secret for a reason, and it was people like Thomas who would look down upon such individuals and their way of life. Etta had at first found it strange, the notion of dressing and acting like a child, but her time spent with Nanny Mae and Papa Philip had changed her feelings about all of it. She missed her own father, but the grief had all but dissolved while she was visiting the chateau. Here at the Maddocks' estate, the sadness loomed above her head like a giant cloud, waiting to unleash its wetness and soak her to the core.

"Did my Uncle Jack not tell you why he sent me away?" Etta asked. Perhaps diverting the question was the best course of action.

"He mentioned his desire to marry you off. It seems no one but I was aware of the betrothal."

"Why is that?" Etta asked.

"Are you questioning the validity of the arrangement?" Thomas asked. His eyes narrowed, and he pushed his chair back from the table. "Get up!" he barked at Etta.

"Excuse me?" She had no idea what she had said or done, but if he was planning to use that strap again, she could not bear it. There was only so much blistering her bottom could take.

"Over my knee."

"What did I do?" Etta asked, placing her fork on the table. Her meal was only half-eaten but any desire to take another bite had disappeared. Her stomach sank. She was not quite sure she would not get sick.

"A woman never questions her husband," Thomas said, his voice shrill as he reached for her arm, dragging her up and out of her seat, pulling her down across his lap.

His grip was strong, and even as she fought to get free, she was no match for his strength. He pulled her over his lap and lifted the hem of her dress, revealing her still blushing bottom from the previous night.

"Please," Etta said, begging to get away. "Do not do this." Her voice was filled with fear and tears dripped down her cheeks as she felt his rough callused palms begin to spank her.

"Butler!" Thomas continued smacking her red cheeks.

"Yes, sir?"

Etta had not seen the gentleman enter the room, and as if it was not horrifying enough to know the stranger could see her bare bottom, Thomas continued to spank her while speaking to him.

"Bring me the paddle. My hand will grow tired after ten or twelve swats."

Etta's eyes widened in horror. She should have been relieved that he was not requesting the strap, but each swat felt more painful than the last, and knowing what was to come only made the pain seep deeper beneath her skin, like a scar that would not go away.

"Please, no!" she cried, her legs kicking and her hips twisting, trying to escape her punishment; one she felt was both harsh and unjustified. She could not see the butler but she could hear his footsteps between smacks to her bare bottom. The burning sizzled through her skin and radiated down her legs as he landed several blows below the plush curves of her buttocks. She would never sit again.

"You will learn that speaking to me in such a tone will not be tolerated," Thomas said. "I am the head of the household. You are nothing more than a woman I have taken in. That will not change when you are my wife."

His harsh statement was met with a painful spank from the paddle.

Etta did not dare answer him. What good would it do? She had lost count of the number of spankings he'd given her. She doubted it would be less than the twenty-five swats with the strap she had endured last night. Perhaps Nanny Joan had a salve she could apply to heal the blistered raw strokes that left marks on her skin. Would she help her, or would Nanny Joan face the same brutality from Thomas? Etta would not wish this on anyone. Not even her worst enemy, which most days was herself.

The wood cracked against her skin, landing on her swollen rear. "I am sorry," she cried, hoping the tears and her apology would be enough to stop Thomas.

The more Etta thought about his wife's death, the more she felt certain that the woman had either died from being spanked too much, or she had run off to protect herself. Though why would any sane woman leave her children behind?

"You will obey me from this moment forward, or I will paddle your bottom every night before bed, in addition to the swats you receive for your poor choices in behavior," Thomas said. "One slip-up during the day and you will get fifteen swats of the paddle when you lie down at night."

"I swear it will not happen again." Etta could not even fathom what she had done that was wrong. Asking seemed like a terrible idea. She would accept her punishment and when Thomas was not looking, she'd get as far from the estate as possible.

The paddle smacked her cheeks again. She clenched on impact and then released her tightened muscles, having learned that being relaxed hurt far less. Though she felt nowhere near relaxed.

"Five more," Thomas said. "If I hear you whimper, it will be ten."

Etta did not answer. She kept her mouth shut and tried to gasp only with the sound of the paddle, blending in her whimpers and moans so that Thomas could not hear the pain he inflicted. Did it upset him to hear her discomfort? She opened her lips, wanted to shout to him to please stop, but the paddle landed for one final swat before he helped her stand.

Her tears had soaked his trousers and the floor. "In the corner. One hour. Keep your dress above your waist!"

Etta walked to the corner of the room, grateful she would not have to see anyone's faces as they witnessed her red sore bottom. She kept her dress at her waist, her hands trembling along with her legs the longer she stood.

Time seemed to tick but at a slow impossible rate, as if the hour would never end.

Eventually it did. "You are dismissed," Thomas said.

Etta sniffled and ran as quickly as she could from the dining room upstairs. She had no money and only the clothes she was wearing. Where would she go? Staying at the estate was not an option. She needed to leave as soon as she could slip away undetected. First, she would talk to Nanny Joan, to ensure that Sophia and Mary were in good hands, untouched and unharmed. If Thomas did anything to hurt his girls in the way he had hurt her, she would whisk them away from their father and protect them, at all costs.

TWENTY

PHILIP RODE through the afternoon and arrived at Jack Waters' residence, giving a firm knock on the door.

An older woman opened it. "Hello. Can I help you, sir?" the housekeeper asked.

"I am here to see Mr. Jack Waters."

"Is he expecting you?" She had graying hair and pale, gray-blue eyes.

"He ought to be." How could he not expect Philip to show up after what occurred at Ashby? One did not just enroll in the school and then leave on a whim, with another man. What made even less sense was the idea that Etta was betrothed to another man.

"Come in," the woman said, opening the front door further to allow him entrance inside.

Philip removed his top hat and coat, offering it to her to hang up.

"Philip," Jack's voice carried from the second story as he descended the stairs. "I am surprised you are here. Is it because I have withdrawn my niece from your finishing school? I know you may have counted on the money, but I assure you that I shall complete payment through the end of the month."

It was not about money, it was about Etta and her well-being—aside from the fact that Philip had grown to love her, and the thought of any other man taking her as their bride, he found repulsive. "I demand to know where she is at once."

"Why should I tell you?" Jack asked. His eyes narrowed and his brow twitched slightly. "The girl is out of both of our hair. Is that not what we both wanted? You needed to find her a husband, and he came to me. It seems she was already to marry the man, though we had no news of it."

"What man?" Philip needed to hear it from the source himself.

"Thomas Maddock came to me just the other day. He showed me the paperwork that Etta's father had signed."

"I wish to see a copy of it," Philip said. Certainly if such a paper existed, Jack would have kept a copy among his things.

"You are mad to think I care about Henrietta and whom she marries. The money speaks louder, and I assure you that Thomas providing half of the estate that she grew up on is enough to satisfy all doubts and nagging curiosities. They are to be wed. No one can stop it," Jack said emphatically.

Philip had every intention of stopping the wedding. There would be no Etta Maddock if it were up to him. He would much rather she took his name of Hartley, though he'd be gentleman enough to give her the choice as to whether she wanted to marry him. Was he worried that she might be happier with Thomas? Of course, but he could not know without chasing her down and finding out the truth.

"Tell me where I can find this Thomas Maddock." It had been why Philip had come to see Jack. If he'd had any knowledge of her whereabouts, he would have skipped this visit entirely. The added fact that

Jack knew and was eager to give her away only made Philip hate the man more. Jack did not care about Etta's well-being, only about marrying her off and getting rid of any responsibility he had toward her. Why had her father entrusted the care of his daughter to Jack? It made little sense.

"He is in the moors, on an estate twice the size of this property," Jack said. "You will have little trouble finding him, he lives not far from the train station, but he will not relinquish Henrietta as easily as you hope." Jack pulled out a map of the railways and pointed to the station closest to the Maddocks' property.

"How do you know all this?" Philip asked.

"The information regarding his estate was on the original papers that Henrietta's father signed declaring she'd marry Thomas. I may have taken a peek for curiosity's sake."

Philip felt quite glad that Jack did at least know where to find Etta. The carriage would be quicker from where he was already located. He'd leave at once to recover his little girl and bring her to Ashby with him again.

"What do you expect to find, Philip?" Jack asked.

"I need to know that she is pleased with Thomas and wants to stay with him." Philip had spent too many hours and sleepless nights thinking about little Etta. He could not abandon her without knowing she wanted to leave Ashby and that she was pleased. Even if she were, would he be able to turn around and return home? Philip did not know the answer. He would find out when he arrived to greet her.

"Very well," Jack said. "I suggest you stay for dinner, the ride is long and the horses could use the rest."

Philip did not disagree. "That would be kind of you." His horses had been riding all day and the journey to the moors would take several more hours. He did not bother to ask about staying the night. He would not feel comfortable, and doubted sleep would find him. He was too concerned about Etta and knowing that she was safe. The sooner he found her, the sooner he'd feel at ease. Until then, he would survive on lack of sleep and his non-existent appetite. He'd get a little nourishment at dinner, but he doubted he could eat a full meal like at home.

Philip found it difficult not to worry about Etta. He always interviewed the papas for the girls at the chateau, making sure they were in the best care possible when they left for good. He had not been given that chance with Thomas, which he found unsettling. The gentleman had swept in, stolen her from the locked hall, and walked her right out of the building. There were supposed to be security measures to ensure the protection of his littles. He knew that would have to be amended when he returned, but his mind dragged back to the men who had requested a little only to be rejected. Was the name Thomas Maddock familiar? Philip could not remember. He just hoped he was not a man who had been turned away and who now sought revenge.

TWENTY-ONE

HER BOTTOM HURT profusely and Etta could not sit down. She lay on her bed, crying until there were no more tears to fall.

"Is everything all right?" Nanny Joan asked after knocking softly.

Etta shook her head, stood, and wiped the snot and tears from her face. "Would you close the door?" she asked, wanting a moment of privacy. She did not want the butler or Thomas to overhear their conversation.

"Of course," Nanny Joan shut the door behind her and stepped closer to Etta. "Do you want to tell me what is wrong? I know Mr. Maddock can be quite intimidating at first, but I assure you he is incredibly fond of you. He would not have brought you into his home and to help with his girls if he did not like you."

That was not enough for Etta. She could not remain in this place. Etta stepped closer to the young plump woman, her voice dropping in case anyone listened from outside. "Does he hurt his girls the way he disciplines me?"

"Do you mean, does he use the strap or paddle? Of course not. I have never seen him lift a hand to either of his girls. Though he also does not pay them much attention, either. They are good girls, Etta. Mary just needs more time with you to warm up. You are not thinking of leaving here already?"

It was not the girls that bothered Etta. She could not handle Thomas. "I cannot stay. Thomas would be better off finding another wife who can make him happy." It was obvious to Etta that she'd only upset him at every juncture. They'd spent less than a day together and he had made her bottom far sorer than it had been her entire stay at Ashby. She wanted to go home, and though she had not known quite where that was, it was beginning to dawn on her.

"You are leaving?" Nanny Joan frowned. "Thomas will not be pleased when he discovers you are missing."

"Swear you will not tell him I am gone. I need him to discover it on his own. Let me have a head start." Etta had to pray that Nanny Joan would not betray her. She'd keep where she intended to go from the young woman, in case she had loose lips.

Nanny Joan dug into her pocket, pulling out a few coins and dropping them into Etta's hand. "This will be enough for your train ride wherever you intend to go. You should leave soon, before Thomas requests your presence for lunch. Head through the gates and keep going. You will eventually reach the station," she whispered furtively.

Lunch was still a few hours away, which meant Etta would have a slight head start before Thomas noticed she'd gone missing. Would she need to worry about him coming after her? What if the train did not leave until noon? No. She needed to leave and would not concern herself with such matters until the time came and she was faced with them head on.

Etta needed to find the Ashby Chateau, but she'd traveled there by carriage in the middle of the night.

How would she discover its location or know which train to take to get there? She did not have anything to pack so she headed quietly down the stairs, giving a brief nod of thanks to the nanny before she slipped out of the front door.

The lawns were dull, the sky gray. The air felt chilly and Etta wrapped her arms around herself to keep warm. She walked along the path made by the carriage as she headed away from the estate toward the train station. Her feet moved swiftly, afraid that at any moment Thomas would look out the window and see Etta in her bright red gown escaping his home. She did not even want to know what the punishment for running away would be. The strap had been for language, and the paddle, well, she could not quite fathom what she'd done that morning to deserve any punishment at all.

In the distance, Etta could make out the dark black silhouette of a carriage and two horses pulling the contraption. Who was heading in this direction? She needed to hide but her dress made it impossible. She scurried toward the nearest hill, climbing over it, and then pressed her body flat against the ground, glancing up over the mound, curious as to who was approaching the estate she'd just run away from.

Etta could not see who sat inside the carriage, whether it was a man or woman. She waited until the carriage was in the farthest reaches, distant and barely visible before she stood up and continued toward the train station. Lifting her feet higher, she picked up the pace, wanting to get there well before the train left. She did not want Thomas coming after her. She needed to be gone on whatever train came through town. It did not matter where it traveled to, she could always rethink her route later, if she could ever discover where Ashby was located.

Etta felt her heart quicken at the sight of the train already waiting at the station. She jogged at a brisk pace, her heels making it difficult but not impossible for her to dash across the platform, grabbing the handrail as the train began to move. She jumped on, gripping the metal, and stepped in through the doors, out of breath.

Taking a few calming drinks of air into her lungs, she walked toward the back of the car and grabbed an empty seat, sitting down. Resting her hands in her lap, her cheeks must have been flushed as a gentleman spun around in his seat, looking her over.

"Nothing like running to catch the train to make you feel alive," he said.

Etta smiled politely. "Yes." It was more than that, but the gentleman old enough to be her father did not need to know about it.

From the window, she watched as the train sped up, the moors passing by at an unprecedented pace. She had never ridden by train before. There had been no need when she had tended to her father. The entire experience was foreign and felt strange but good.

"Where are you going?" the gentleman asked, continuing to make polite conversation with her. He stood up, moving from his seat to sit across from her.

Etta wished she had not said anything at all. A simple answer of 'yes' had surely made him think she was open to having a discussion. What would she say to ward off any doubts? "I am visiting a friend," she said. It was an easy lie, so long as she did not have to elaborate as to where. She did not even know where the train was taking her.

His brown eyes crinkled and he smiled warmly at her. "I am on my way home to visit my girls and my wife. I have had some business to attend to."

"How long since you have last seen them?" Etta asked, trying to make polite conversation while also steering the topic away from herself. She relaxed as she spoke to him, feeling slightly more at ease.

"It has been three months."

"That is surprising." She had not expected anyone to be away from their family for so long. "May I ask why?" She tried to remember her manners. She'd spent far too much time looking after her ailing father and then at the chateau to remember what it was like to be a grown up.

"I work for the coastguard."

"What's that like?" Etta knew he must have spent months at a time at sea. It seemed dreadful to leave his family behind.

"Not bad if you do not get seasick," he said, quirking a grin.

"I take it you have a rock hard stomach?" Etta was not sure how she'd be on the water. She'd never been, and hoped never to find out, either. She could not swim, so what good would it do to travel near water?

"Like you would not believe."

The train slowed and Etta's eyes widened as she glanced out of the window. "Why are we stopping?" she asked. Her voice sounded frantic and she wiped her sweaty hands on her dress. Thomas could not have forced them to stop the train, could he have? He had quite a bit of money, but did he have the resources necessary to make such demands?

"We are at the next station," the gentleman said. "You have never taken the train before, have you?"

"Is it that obvious?" She laughed softly, staring down at her hands in her lap. She had worried for nothing. Etta had managed to escape Thomas, she had no reason to worry about him tracking her down. He would not know where she disembarked the train, and she would not remain at the station to help him figure it out, either.

TWENTY-TWO

PHILIP RODE THROUGH THE NIGHT, letting his coachman drive while he slept in the carriage. It had not been comfortable, and he wondered how Etta had managed to fall asleep beside him that night not so long ago.

As he rubbed his tired eyes, the morning light streamed in, and he looked out of the window as they rode through the moors. He'd given his coachman directions to the destination—though he had not known exactly where Thomas Maddock lived, he'd used the map to locate his whereabouts. He would find Etta, and when he did, hopefully she would be glad to see him. If she was not pleased, it might actually break his heart.

Philip's stomach grumbled and he wished he'd have taken some food with him aside from having had dinner at Jack's home. He had not eaten much, having been too concerned about Etta. Now that was taking its toll, causing him to be tired and even more hungry as nausea set in.

Resting his eyes momentarily, he relaxed until he felt a bump jolt him fully upright and awake. Glancing outside to see what the fuss was about, he noticed there were a few rocks and hills, but nothing that should have caused such a stir. The carriage continued moving without delay. At least there had not been any damage to the undercarriage or wheels from whatever they had hit.

From the corner of his gaze, he caught sight of a glimmer of red, just over the hill. His eyes narrowed as he tried to examine what he was seeing, uncertain what could stand out so much in a sea of winter grass, dormant and dull.

The gray sky, filled with clouds, stretched on as far as Philip could see. The air grew chilly, far more so than the previous night. Would it snow? He hoped that if it did, it would not be more than a light dusting. He intended to be on his way as soon as he saw Etta, and hopefully she'd accompany him back home.

Rubbing his hands together to keep them warm, he shut the curtain for the carriage, keeping the cool air out. It darkened the small confined space but that never bothered him. There was enough light through the sheer fabric to give the impression of daylight still.

"We are almost there!" the coachman shouted to Philip from outside.

The gentleman must have been chilly, but he'd bundled up far warmer with gloves and a scarf. Philip had not found those items necessary when he'd left the chateau but the weather did change constantly without notice.

His stomach felt as though it were on fire. Was it the lack of food, or the fear that was creeping up on him? What if Etta slammed the door in his face? It would not have been the first time he'd disappointed a young woman, although Etta was the first he had loved. He'd intended to marry her, and he had not changed his mind since the day he met her. His feelings had grown stronger, and he prayed she felt the same way.

The coach pulled to a halt and Philip waited for the coachman to open the door, knowing it was safe to step outside.

A few snowflakes drifted from the sky, one landing on his cheek. He brushed the cold dampness aside and stalked up to the front step of the estate.

Thomas Maddock had no doubt done well for himself. His home was quite elegant from the outside, not as large as the chateau, but impressive all the same, with two stories of brick. It wasn't the height so much as the width of the house, it seemed to extend beyond that of a typical property.

Philip knocked with a brisk force, wanting to be quick with introductions and invited inside.

There was no answer.

He grabbed the handle and tried the door, shifting on his feet. His hands were growing red and numb, the cold seeming unbearable the longer he knocked using the metal handle to jar the attention of someone inside.

From behind the wooden door, he heard the heavy pound of footsteps and then a sequence of clicks to the lock.

"May I help you?" a gentleman answered.

"I am looking for Etta Waters."

The man frowned. "You are searching for Mr. Maddock's betrothed. She is upstairs, I believe. Come on inside."

Philip stepped inside the large home, his coachman right behind him in the foyer.

"Can I help you?" A second gentleman in dark trousers and matching vest came down the stairs. "I am Thomas Maddock. If you have something to say to Etta, you will do it through me."

Philip grimaced. He had not even considered that he would not be allowed to speak with her. "What is it you see in Miss Waters?" Philip asked. "It is certainly not that you two have known each other, because if that were the case, surely she would have known about the arrangement of marriage."

"I do not know what you mean," Thomas said, approaching the stranger standing by the door. "What is it to you?"

"I am Philip Hartley," he said. "The headmaster of the Ashby Chateau, the finishing school you withdrew Etta from without my permission."

"I did not realize permission was needed, considering she is to be my wife." Thomas stood toe-to-toe with Philip.

Philip did not so much as blink. "She was brought in by her uncle's admission, Jack Waters. He is the only one allowed to withdraw her from my care. I demand to see her at once, to know that she is in good health and well cared for before leaving."

Thomas balled his hands into fists. "What business is it of yours?"

"It is my business when you snatch a young girl from my school! A decent gentleman would provide me with the paperwork to prove that you are her guardian and that you will be removing her from my institution. What you did constitutes kidnapping."

"That is insane," Thomas said, his eyes narrowing as he spun around, heading for the stairs. "She is up in her room. You can speak with her, but I must be present. I cannot have her consorting with any men without a chaperone. It would not be appropriate."

"Of course," Philip said. He followed Thomas up the stairwell and down the hall.

"Etta." Thomas knocked on the closed bedroom door. "There is someone here to speak with you. Open the door."

When there was no response, Thomas turned the silver handle and pushed the bedroom door open, revealing an empty bed and quiet room.

"Where is she, Mr. Maddock?" Philip asked, his temper rising.

"I am sure she is around somewhere with the girls. Nanny Joan!" Thomas barked for the girls' attendant as he stormed down the stairs to the playroom.

"Yes, Mr. Maddock?" Nanny Joan stepped out from the room with the children, closing the door behind her to protect the little ones.

"Where is Etta? Is she in there with you?" Thomas asked.

"No, sir." Nanny Joan shook her head. "The girls are playing quietly. Have you checked outside? Or perhaps asked the governess? I do remember Etta mentioning that she'd like to pick up a few gowns of her own."

Thomas ignored the nanny's suggestions. He opened every hall closet and door, searching for the young lady who had gone missing. "Etta! I swear, when I find you—"

"You will what?" Philip asked, watching Thomas very closely. He would not let anyone hurt Etta, not so long as he was alive.

"The devil needs to be beaten out of her. Running away, hiding from me. How am I expected to marry a woman who keeps such secrets?" Thomas' cheeks burned. "I will not have any of it!"

"Perhaps you should not marry her," Philip said. It seemed now was as good a time as any to try and remind Thomas that Etta was more than just a girl on a piece of paper. She meant something to him, and if Thomas did not love her, then she deserved better.

"Excuse me?" Thomas spun around on his heels. "What do you know about it?"

"I know that Etta spent time at the chateau and never once attempted to hide or run away. You must have done something awful to make her feel so frightened."

"She is soft. It will take time to break the young girl in." Thomas walked toward the back door. Opening it, he peered outside. "It is freezing. She could not have gone far."

"What was she wearing this morning?" Philip asked. "I assume you saw her this morning?" Could he have seen Etta without even realizing it on his carriage ride to the estate?

"A red dress that had been my late wife's. Dark red, the color of blood."

"It sounds lovely," Philip said and sighed. "I see that she is gone. My suggestion would be to find yourself a new wife. One who has the desire to stick around for longer than a day." Philip headed for the door, his coachman sitting in the foyer. "It is time to go."

The coachman stood and followed Philip outside. He waited until the door was shut before approaching the gentleman with gloves and a scarf. It was amazing how he could remember all the littles' names, but when it came to staff, Philip knew he failed in many regards. "Sir. Take me back on the road we came, but keep following it as far as you can. Do not turn off and head south. The girl we are searching for—I think I saw her running away."

"Yes, sir." The man helped Philip into the coach. "If I may speak freely, sir?"

"Yes, of course."

"There is a train station not too far from here. If I were a young woman and running away, I would try and make it to the train station."

Apparently his coachman had heard far more than he thought.

"Thank you. To the train station it is," Philip said, sitting down. Though it was chilly outside, he raised the curtain, wanting to see if he spotted Etta on the way. It had been hours since he had caught the glimpse of crimson. Certainly by now she would have caught a train, but where would she have headed? He'd have to check the station and schedules when they arrived. Perhaps all hope was not lost. Philip would find her and she would come back with him to the chateau. It was in her best interest; he would not take no for an answer.

TWENTY-THREE

"THIS IS MY STOP," the gentleman sitting across from Etta said.

The train slowed and he stood, grabbing his bag and glancing out of the window, presumably looking for his family.

"Enjoy your time with your family."

"Thank you. Enjoy visiting with your friend," he said, placing the hat back atop his head. He nodded politely at her as he shuffled down the aisle to the doors. The train pulled to a stop and he stepped off, his bag in hand, walking down the platform toward his wife and children who were standing there attentive and excited to see him.

Etta watched from the window as he embraced his wife and two children in his arms. She shifted, glancing away; the moment felt too personal, as though she was intruding. Shutting her eyes, she realized she did not know where the end of the line would take her. Reading the map would have been easy if she knew where she had started and what train she was on. Instead it felt like interpreting a foreign language, something she was incapable of doing.

The train lurched forward and Etta relaxed, something she had not done in quite some time. Though her bottom burned profusely as she sat, standing for such a long time as the train jolted forward and to the side seemed dangerous. Perhaps she'd grown numb in some ways from the blistered bottom she'd received while with Thomas. She would never see him again.

"Is this seat taken?"

Etta's eyes flashed open, recognizing the familiar voice and smell as he did not wait for her to answer. He took a seat opposite her, staring deep into her eyes. "Philip?" she asked, surprised to see him on the train. Had she been dreaming? A lot had happened lately, perhaps she'd grown delirious in her current state.

"Yes, little Etta."

She smiled, surprised he did not mention punishing her for not calling him 'Papa'. As strong as Philip was, he was not mean or abusive. He had been kind to her, far kinder than any other man she'd met. "How did you find me?" she asked.

"Not easily," he said. He relaxed as he sat across from her. "I paid a visit to your Uncle Jack last night. He informed me of your betrothal to Thomas Maddock."

Etta made a face of disgust. She sneered at the gentleman's name. "I am not marrying him."

Philip sighed. Was he relieved or disappointed to hear the news? "Why did you leave Ashby with him?" he asked.

"I did not have a choice. Nanny Beth released me into his care. I did not want to go. I even told her so!" A small part of her wanted nothing to do with Nanny Beth, but that had been before she knew what Thomas was really like.

"And now what do you want?"

"I want to go back to Ashby, Philip. I want to be your little one. Can I have that?" She knew it may be too late. She'd run off, and though it had not been entirely her doing, she perhaps had lost his trust as well. Besides, she'd got Nanny Mae fired, was he not angry with her about that, too?

He leaned forward, his hand finding hers. "What do you call me?"

"Papa," she answered, keeping her voice down, though the train car was not entirely full. No one could hear what they said.

"That is my good little Etta." Philip nodded. "Come and sit with me," he said, patting his lap.

She glanced around the carriage. Would anyone think it highly inappropriate for a grown woman to be sitting on his lap?

"Etta." His voice grew stern and she stood, shaking slightly as she lowered herself down onto his lap. His arms wrapped around her waist, pulling her close, cuddling her. She heard him breathe deeply. Was he relieved to have found her?

"What will happen with regards to Thomas?" Etta asked. "I am promised to him, but I do not wish to marry him." Could Philip help her out of the betrothal? "He's a horrible man, Papa. He blistered my bottom for no reason at all this morning."

Philip nodded slowly. Whether he believed her or not, he did not say. "You do not have to concern yourself with Thomas any longer."

"What about the documents he had?" she asked. "He had papers drawn up that said I was to be his wife. My father signed them."

"It is easy to forge a signature, little one. We do not know for a fact that he was not conning you out of your estate money and dowry."

Etta paused, considering Papa's words. It was possible, though Thomas had money and it did not seem as if he needed more; perhaps it had come from the other guests who had stayed for a short time, as well. Unfortunately she would no longer be able to ask Nanny Joan any more questions. She would have to trust that Thomas would leave her be and move on. Were there any guarantees that he would not come back for her?

Philip ran his fingers through her long blonde hair, pushing the strands out of her eyes. "What is wrong, my little love?"

"What if he does return and insists I marry him?" It seemed her Uncle Jack did not care whom she wed, and so long as he was still in charge of her dowry, Thomas could claim her as his wife.

"It will be too late," Philip said. "Which is why I want us to wed."

Etta's eyes lit up. "You want to marry me? Even after the trouble I caused to Nanny Mae?"

His hand smoothed over her back. "Nanny Mae is the cause of her own trouble. You are not responsible for her actions."

She certainly felt responsible. "What happens after we get married?" Etta asked. "Will I still be a little at the chateau?"

"You will always be my little Etta," he said, kissing her cheek. "You will stay at Ashby a little longer, until you have learned to fully submit, at which point you will come home with me."

Her heart skipped a beat, excitement bubbling inside her. "You do not live at the chateau?" she asked. It made sense that he lived elsewhere, but he always seemed to be around, unlike the other papas.

"No, darling." He kissed her temple. "You are the only reason I stayed well beyond my typical hours. I look forward to putting you to bed. We missed that bedtime story."

Etta smiled. "Yes, we did." She did not mind being little—not when it involved Philip, who gave her the opportunity to be child-like and carefree.

With one hand wrapped snugly around her waist, he nuzzled her neck. "Tell me something, and please be honest with me."

"Of course." She had no reason to lie to him.

"How did you feel with Thomas?"

"I hated him!" How could Papa ask her such a question? Thomas had blistered her bottom and punished her at every opportunity and then some.

"I meant living there, with children who needed tending to."

"Are you asking me what I thought of being a mother? I spent five minutes with the girls. Mary hated me. It definitely did not make me anxious to have children."

"But do you want them?" Philip asked.

Etta frowned, not understanding the question. "I do not know." Was it terrible that she was not thrilled at the idea of having children? She did not want to push Philip away. "Why are you asking me this, Papa?" She used the name he preferred to be called, trying to understand where his mind was heading. What was he thinking?

"I need to know if you will be upset if we never have children."

"Oh." She let out a soft breath. "Can I be honest?"

"That is all I have ever wanted from you," Papa said. He held her close, his breath mingling with hers.

"I spent years caring for my sick father. I am not sure I have it in me to raise a child. It is probably selfish, and I am sure one day it will happen, but the thought is terrifying and repulsive to me at the moment."

A smile grew across his lips. "Repulsive?"

"You wanted honesty." Was he regretting asking her?

Papa laughed and nodded. "Yes, I did say you should be honest. I wanted to know how you felt, Etta, because I cannot have children. I am sterile."

"You had the mumps as a child?" Etta guessed. She'd heard of such instances of men being unable to father children due to the disease.

"I was fifteen at the time."

"Oh." She pulled back slightly to look into his eyes. "Is that why you have Ashby?"

"I have Ashby so that I could meet you."

Though his words were sweet, she knew that was not the case. "I heard you were married, a long time ago?"

Papa shifted slightly, unable to move too much since she was sitting on his lap. The train swayed and he glanced briefly out of the window. "My late wife passed away in childbirth," he said quietly.

"But I thought you just said—"

"She was not pregnant with my child," Papa said. "She was two months pregnant when we met. Claire fell in love with a nobleman. He refused to leave his wife and did not care that he'd ruined her reputation. I met her at the tavern and stepped in, offered to marry her, and help raise the child as my own."

"Why would you do that?" Etta asked. She did not understand why he'd wed a complete stranger.

"I had had a little too much to drink," he said, joking with her. "She was a nice girl, her family had disowned her. In the couple of hours I spent talking to Claire, I felt something for her. I knew I could not ever have a child and the notion of helping her raise her son or daughter brought me joy."

"What happened to the child?"

"Claire had a baby boy, but he died with her while she was in labor. It was a sad day."

Etta's hand gently stroked his cheek. She had not meant to upset him by talking about it. "I am so sorry for your loss." She meant every word she spoke. She may have been glad that he was not married and could be with her, but she never would have wanted him to go through such a horrific ordeal. No one deserved to lose the people they loved, especially two of them on the same day.

"Thank you," he said, moving her hand from his cheek to his lips. He kissed her palm. "It is what made me desire to create Ashby. I wanted a home both for young women who needed to learn how to behave properly, and also a secret lair of my own."

The smile spread across Etta's face. "Is that what you are calling the littles' school?"

"What would you prefer I call it?" he asked.

She shrugged. She did not have an answer. The idea still felt fresh and new to her, but she looked forward to returning, even if it would not be for a while.

The train pulled to a halt. He patted her back. "Stand up. This is our stop."

"It is?" She glanced out of the window as she stood.

Papa headed down the aisle for the door. "Etta," he said, calling for her to join him.

She dashed down the aisle, catching up as the train stopped and the doors opened. He stepped out into the cold and she followed. The brisk air swirled around her. She wrapped her arms around herself, chilled in her short sleeves. The long dress did not do her any favors either, with the thin silk material blowing in the wind.

"Come now," Philip said, grabbing Etta's hand. He led her from the platform and across the light dusting of snow toward a carriage. "Thank you for meeting us."

The coachman nodded and opened the door, offering his hand to Etta.

She climbed in and Papa removed his jacket, wrapping it around her shoulders to keep her warm.

TWENTY-FOUR

THE RIDE back to Ashby was quiet. Etta had fallen asleep once again on Philip's shoulder. He loved the warmth of her body beside him, and he kept his arm nestled around her, keeping her close to him.

She stirred as the coach slowed. "Are we back already?"

Philip did not point out that she'd been asleep for hours. He envied how peaceful she had looked. "I need you to do me a favor," he said. He had been wondering when to tell her about the task he required of her. There were few people he trusted more than Etta. She had come back to him, which meant he could trust her and love her openly.

"Of course, what is it?" she asked. Etta rubbed the sleep from her eyes and yawned. She still appeared to be half asleep.

Glancing out of the window, he could see the chateau in the distance. He needed to ask her now, before it was too late. "You are friends with Leda, correct?"

She nodded. "Yes. I suppose so."

"I need you to tell me if she is being a good girl or whether she is planning something naughty. Do you think you can handle that?" Philip asked.

"You want me to tattle on Leda?" Etta asked.

Philip cringed. He had not meant it to sound so cruel but how could he trust that Leda was being a good girl and had learned to submit? She'd been tricking them, and he needed someone he could count on to discover the truth. "I want you to observe your friend's behavior and if you think she is not being honest or real, then yes, you will tell me."

Etta stared at him for a long moment. Was she deciding whether or not to obey his request? "Leda told me that she knew how to get out of the chateau;

by pretending to submit to her papa," she said at length.

It was exactly what Philip already knew. "How does that make you feel?"

"Terrible! I would never do that. You are so good to me. I want to please you and submit to you. Leda is not a very nice person. Why is she still there?"

"Sometimes good girls do naughty things," Philip said, trying to remind Etta that Leda was not a bad person; she just needed a steady dose of discipline and submission.

"Why do you not let her go? If she is not pleased with her papa, surely someone else can make him happy."

It was a very good point. He sighed, pulling her closer as he hugged her to him. "Maybe we should talk about that with Papa Francis." The man would not be pleased, but he could most certainly find another little willing to please him and love him as he desired from Leda.

The coachman pulled the carriage to the front of the chateau and stepped around to open the door. He offered a hand to Etta, helping her down onto the slippery steps that were covered in a thin layer of ice and snow.

Philip grabbed her arm, helping her walk up the steps and inside, making sure she did not fall. He walked with her into the littles' hall and led her to her nursery room.

Standing outside the door, she sighed, slipping his jacket off her shoulders and handing it to him. "I suppose playtime is over."

It was clear to him that she had enjoyed her time away from the chateau. He would need to do that more with her; take her places and show her the world.

"Come now." He gently patted her back. "It is time to get your night clothes on, wash your face, and Nanny Beth will read you a bedtime story."

Etta sighed but she did not fight him.

"What is it?" he asked, sensing her discomfort. "You do not like Nanny Beth?" It was not a hard guess to make, seeing as how the woman had relinquished Etta into Thomas's care.

"I miss Nanny Mae," Etta said. She glanced toward the bedroom, avoiding her Papa's eyes.

"Is that all?" His thumb reached under her chin, bringing her to look into his steady gaze.

"Will you read me a bedtime story?" she asked.

Philip was tired, but he could not say no to his little Etta. "How about we get you ready for bed together? Just you and me?"

Her eyes lit up and she nodded vigorously.

Etta headed into her nursery and Philip followed, closing the door behind them. "Take off that dress. It is not appropriate for a little girl."

"But I like it," she said, twirling around.

"And one day, when you graduate from Ashby, you will have an assortment of dresses for the right occasion."

"Will I no longer be a little when we are married?" she asked.

"You will always be my little Etta, but there will be times when it is appropriate, and times when you will be expected to act properly, as a lady would." He did not want to lie to her. He would have loved to keep her little forever, but it was not truly possible. "Tonight you are my little one." He walked to the armoire and removed a soft teal gown for bed. "You will wear this after I give you your plug."

Etta swallowed, her eyes on him the entire time. "I am not sure my bottom can take it."

He walked over, helping her remove the gown as she lifted her arms and he pulled the red layers of fabric over her head and let them fall to the floor. She turned around, letting him see her bottom.

"Did he do this to you?" Philip asked. Anger boiled in his veins at the thought of anyone touching his little Etta.

She sighed. "It is why I ran off this morning. I could not take any more of his discipline."

Philip shook his head. In all the years he'd disciplined his girls, he had never seen such brutality and lack of restraint. "This will not ever happen again. Spankings are meant to teach and hurt while the lesson is taught, but not days or weeks later." He knew that sitting on the train and in the coach must have been awful for her. She'd held herself well, showing very little evidence of discomfort. Just touching her bottom would be horribly painful for her. Philip did not want her to think he was the same sort of monster that Thomas was. He would show her how different he was.

"Your plug can wait until your bottom has healed."

"Thank you, Papa." She spun around, letting him see her naked breasts and quim.

Philip swallowed, arousal coursing through his body at just seeing her naked. His breath found her lips and he kissed her softly, his fingers moving between her thighs as she parted her legs for him. "Climb onto the bed," he whispered between kisses.

"What about my nightgown?" she asked.

"You do not need it."

Clothes were the furthest thing from his mind. He climbed above Etta, towering over her as his lips descended back down onto hers.

She wrapped her hands around him, tugging at his shirt, scraping her nails under his clothes.

He should have pinned her down, proven that they were not equals and he was in charge, but damn, they'd been through so much after he thought he had lost her. All he could think about was her pussy pulsating around his rock hard cock.

His kisses traveled down her torso and across her stomach in soft light movements as he parted her thighs and let his breath tingle against her wetness. Already she was soaked, and he could smell her sweet aroma that made his cock twitch in his trousers.

She moaned as his tongue grazed her quim, and his nose nuzzled the tiny bead that had reddened and begun to swell under his ministrations. His fingers slipped into her warmth, stroking as he licked her clit, grazing each side, listening to her sounds and watching the flush spread across her body.

"Papa," she moaned, further eliciting excitement from Philip as her eyes squeezed shut. He quickened his movements as he felt her tightening around his digits, her insides swelling, about ready to explode as her toes curled and her body tightened around him, clenching her legs together as much as possible. He steadied her with one hand, the other continuing to stroke her. His tongue teased her bud as she shuddered beneath him.

Gasping for air, Etta slowly opened her eyes, staring down at him. Her hands reached for his shirt, pulling it up and over his head. Her skin was warm but this time he knew why as he crawled up her torso, covering her in soft sweet kisses.

"Take off your trousers," Etta said. She then tugged at the cotton undergarment beneath them. "Everything off."

Philip pinned her down, his breath teasing her, refusing to kiss her. "Who is in charge?" he asked, reminding her that he was the boss and she was to submit to him.

"I know. I know. Let me do this for you, all right?" Her hands traveled down his stomach and reached for his cock, taking it into her hand, her fingers stroking the length. She guided him onto his back and then she climbed around, straddling him as she leaned down, taking his glistening shaft into her mouth.

His fingers tangled in her hair as he felt her tongue graze the head of his cock, forcing his insides to tighten and swell. She sparked something in him that he had not realized had been dormant.

Her lips moved along his length, sucking and licking the shaft, taking him deeper inside her throat.

Philip's eyes slammed shut and one hand stayed planted in her hair, the other tangling in the bed sheets as he tried not to hurt her. He could not remember the last time a woman had willingly serviced him in this manner. The littles he disciplined—but he never rewarded them with sexual behavior. That had been strictly left up to their papas. He'd been missing out for years on what another woman could give to him. Etta had restored his faith in love. His heart pounded against his ribcage as she took him into the back of her throat. Not even his wife had been able to do that. It was a skill they taught to the littles, and it took time to master. Etta apparently was a natural.

She hummed softly, and the vibrations and her soft thrusts were enough to send him over the edge.

He grunted and moaned; an attempt to warn her about what was to follow. She kept her mouth around his cock, swallowing the liquid as it poured into her throat and down her chin. Etta licked up every drop, wiping the remains around her lips.

Philip gasped, collapsing onto the bed, shocked that he had not even asked her to swallow, yet she'd done it on her own. "Have you ever—" He wanted to know if that had been the first time she'd done that.

Blushing, she shook her head. "Just for you. I hope I did all right?"

He grinned. She did not need to worry. For a beginner, she'd been skilled, and it made his heart throb and cock threaten to twitch at the mere thought that if that was a first, what else could she be good at that they had not tried? Were there new possibilities that he had not considered? He was well versed in submission and sex, but perhaps Etta knew something he did not.

"You did amazingly," he said, lying down on the bed, pulling her to lie with him. His fingers smoothed over her hips and across her stomach. Just staring at her naked body was making him crave a second round.

TWENTY-FIVE

ALL SHE WANTED to do was please him. Philip had been kind and generous to her, firm yet loving. He had opened her to new experiences and showed her a world she had never imagined possible.

"I do not want to wait until we are married," Etta said.

"What is that?" Papa asked.

"I want you to take my purity," she whispered, not wanting anyone else to overhear her words. Her fingers moved down his stomach and between his legs, reaching for his cock.

"Etta, that is something I believe should only happen after we marry."

"Then marry me tonight," she said, her eyes dark and filled with longing. She had had a taste and desired more.

"We cannot. Even if I wanted to, and I do, it is not possible."

She leaned in, brushing her lips over his. "I do not care." If he would not marry her tonight, then he could satisfy the throbbing that had built once again between her thighs. Etta reached for his hand, dragging it across the folds of her wetness, letting him feel the need building inside her.

Philip kissed her, pushing his tongue past her lips, rolling her onto her back as he shoved his knee against the juncture of her parted thighs.

She opened her mouth to ask him what he was doing when she felt him rock against her, the pressure overwhelming and seemingly insatiable. Etta moaned, her head lolling back with her neck exposed, and her papa leaned in, kissing the milky white skin, licking and sucking as he trailed a path of wet kisses down her breasts.

"I want to feel you inside me." She craved more than just his tongue and fingers. What they had done thus far had been great but not enough.

Her hand moved down between them, finding his cock, her fingers grazed the tip and stroked the shaft as he grew under her touch.

His lips above her heart paused as she aroused him, his fingers pulling tighter against her hips, the need building between them. He pushed her hand away and guided his own hand down to his cock, positioning himself at her entrance.

"Spread your legs," he said, instructing her on what to do.

Etta shifted her legs further apart.

He towered above her, the head of his cock glistening as he inched it inside her tight entrance.

She moaned, already he was stretching her and he'd barely pushed inside her quim. Slowly he moved with more intensity, causing her lips to part and a cry to expel from her mouth as he pushed past her maidenhead.

Philip covered her lips, tangled his legs with hers and rolled her slightly to the side, spanking her raw bottom.

Etta whimpered, the pain no longer radiating in her quim but on her backside. Her tight muscles seemed to relax as he drew his cock most of the way out before sliding back inside her tight canal, guiding her once again onto her back.

Her fingers trailed over his skin and down his torso, her nails burying in his rear as he continued to thrust and grind his hips into hers. Her body felt as though it were on fire. The burn was negligible compared to the throbbing pulsating sensation she felt as he filled her. Etta found his lips, needing to taste him with kisses, drinking him in, the smell of sex surrounding them as her toes curled.

He dipped his fingers down to her clit, two digits rubbing over the swollen pearl. Her body tightened around his cock, shuddering as she moaned, unraveling around him.

Philip pushed harder and faster, letting himself go along with her, soaking her cunny with his seed. Gingerly he slid from her quim and untangled himself from her embrace. Panting and gasping for air, he sat up, perched on the edge of the bed. After a moment of catching his breath, he leaned down to pick up his clothes.

Etta sat up in bed, confused. "Where are you going, Papa?"

"Nowhere. I just do not think it is appropriate for anyone to see us both lying naked when Nanny Beth comes in."

"You care what she thinks?" Etta asked and laughed. It was the most absurd thing she'd heard since arriving at Ashby.

Her papa sighed. "We have a reputation to uphold."

"Do you love me?" she asked, her voice soft and tentative. If Philip was to marry her, then her reputation at Ashby made very little difference. Besides, the outside world had no idea what went on behind the closed doors of Ashby. Unless Nanny Beth blabbed about it—and Etta suspected that would be against the rules—then she had nothing to worry about.

"Yes, of course." He turned around to face her.

"Then I do not care what Nanny Beth or anyone thinks," Etta said. "I want you to stay with me."

Philip pulled his cotton underpants back on and then drew back the covers, joining Etta to lie down.

He wrapped his arms around her, the sheets keeping them warm along with each other.

————

Philip had felt bad, untangling himself from Etta's warm comfortable embrace as morning arrived. He had work to do and needed to check on how everything had been while he was away.

He crept out of bed and took his trousers and shirt from the floor, putting the clothes back on before slipping from her room. He tried to be quiet with the door, not wanting to stir her awake. She'd had quite a long day away from the chateau.

"You are back," Nanny Beth said, coming down the hall, catching sight of him exiting Etta's room.

He hoped she had not noticed that he was wearing the same clothing as he had the previous day. "Yes. Etta is asleep. I suggest you let her get some rest. It is been a tough couple of days on her. When she wakes up, get her breakfast and then send her to the playroom with Leda." He still needed to know what was going on with little Leda. Was she coming around after her recent discipline, or did she perhaps need to be let go, sent into the world on her own, without her papa to look after her?

Philip paid Nanny Vivian a visit, making sure she was handling Gracie all right. Gracie had taken time to adjust but she was not the problem child that little Leda had become. Each girl had her own unique personality. He had to remind himself of that every time a new young woman was brought into the school as a little.

The morning drudged by the more he thought about Etta. At around mid-morning, he headed into the playroom, hoping that Etta had spent some time with Leda. Philip watched from the window. Etta did not seem pleased. Had Leda told her something that had upset her? He waited several minutes, watching the exchange before Etta walked up to Nanny Beth and whispered something into her ear. Nanny Beth's eyes seemed to meet Philip's, though she could not see him. He swallowed nervously and watched as Nanny Beth stood, taking Etta by the hand as she led her out of the room.

"Papa!" Etta's eyes lit up. She rushed toward him, throwing her arms around him.

Philip wrapped his arms around his little one. "How are you getting along with Leda?"

"All right, I guess. Her papa told her that she could leave and not marry him if that is what she desires. Do you know what she did?"

"What?" Philip asked, surprised that Papa Francis had the willpower to relinquish absolute control.

"She stayed. Leda told me that she is too afraid to leave, to be an adult again. It is why she acts out and causes so much trouble. If she marries her papa and leaves the chateau, she is worried she will have to grow up. It is why she told me about pretending so she could get away. Leda's devious but it is only because she wants to be loved."

Philip breathed a sigh of relief. He kissed Etta's forehead. "I have a present for you in my office. Would you like to come and see it?"

Etta's eyes twinkled and she nodded vigorously, excited.

He took her by the hand and led her to his study. "You can wait out here," he said to Nanny Beth. Leading Etta inside, he pointed to a large brown box perched on his desk, big enough to hold a top hat.

"For you, my little one." He took the box from the desk and handed it to Etta.

She sat down on the couch, opening the box on her lap, revealing a perfectly sewn rag doll. "Is this for me?" she asked. All the toys in the playroom were to be shared and left in there.

"Yes," Philip said and smiled. "For my little Etta. You have your own dolly to hug at night when I am not beside you." He kissed her forehead. "How about we go back into the playroom? You can bring your new friend with you and show her to Leda and Gracie."

"Won't they be jealous?" Etta asked.

"If they know what is good for them, they will be pleased for you and behave."

Etta wrapped her arms around her papa, giving him another hug. "Thank you," she said, kissing his cheek. "You have made me the happiest girl alive."

It was exactly what he had wanted, to love and cherish her, make her completely his, and he had done exactly that.

The End

SHOP ALLISON WEST

SURPRISE! Allison West also writes steamy slow burn romances under the pen name Willow Fox.

If you love signed paperbacks and exclusive content, be sure to check out my website where I have eBooks and paperbacks under all my pen names: https://shopwillowfox.com

SHOP EXCLUSIVE BOOK BOXES & MERCHANDISE

THANK you so much for reading Little Etta! I hope you enjoyed the novel. I absolutely loved writing it.

If you love signed paperbacks and exclusive content, be sure to check out my website: https://shopwillowfox.com

ABOUT THE AUTHOR

Allison West has loved writing since she was in high school (many ages ago). Her small town romances are reflective of living in a small town in rural America.

Whether she's writing romance or sitting outside by the bonfire reading a good book, Willow loves the magic of the written word.

She writes under a variety of pen names including Willow Fox.

Visit her website at:

https://authorwillowfox.com

ALSO BY ALLISON WEST

Gem Apocalypse Series

Emerald Rebellion

Amber Voyeur

Sapphire Sacrifice

Scarlet Assassin

Crimson Crown

Royally Claimed Series

Palace Secrets

Maiden Claimed

Grave Misfortune

Historical Gems

Little Etta: Little Lessons

Little Gigi: Little Lessons

Little Eliza: Little Lessons

Little Kat

Little Lizzie

Little Delia

Want more spice and steam? I also write under the pen name Willow Fox. Those books are often slow-burn but hot!

Eagle Tactical Series

Expose: Jaxson

Stealth: Mason

Conceal: Lincoln

Covert: Jayden

Truce: Declan

Mafia Marriages

Secret Vow

Captive Vow

Savage Vow

Unwilling Vow

Ruthless Vow

Bratva Brothers

Brutal Boss

Wicked Boss

Possessive Boss

Obsessive Boss

Dangerous Boss

Bossy Single Dad Series

Billionaire Grump

Mountain Grump

Bachelor Grump

Ice Dragons Hockey Romance

Faking it with the Billionaire

Daring the Hockey Player

Arresting the Hockey Player

Prefer a sweeter romance with action and adventure?
Check out these titles under the name Ruth Silver.

Aberrant Series

Love Forbidden

Secrets Forbidden

Magic Forbidden

Escape Forbidden

Refuge Forbidden

Boxsets

Nightblood

Royal Reaper

Reaper Academy: Alt Spicy Edition

Standalones

Stolen Art